LOVE AND PROTECT

ELITE FORCE SECURITY
BOOK 3

CHRISTINA TETREAULT

Love And Protect ©2022 by Christina Tetreault
Published by Christina Tetreault
Cover Designer: Amanda Walker
Editing: Hot Tree Editing
Proofreading: Hot Tree Editing

All rights reserved. No part of this book may be reproduced in any form or by any electronic or mechanical means, including information storage and retrieval systems—except in the case of brief quotations embodied in critical articles or reviews—without permission in writing from the author. This book is a work of fiction. The characters, events, and places portrayed in this book are products of the author's imagination and are either fictitious or are used fictitiously. Any similarity to real persons, living or dead, is purely coincidental and not intended by the author. For more information on the author and her works, please see www.christinatetreault.com

Digital ISBN 978-1-7352976-9-9

Print ISBN: 979-8-9865744-0-0

CAST OF CHARACTERS

- **Keith Wallace**
- **Madison Dempsey (Mad Dog)**
- **Lyle Cardi**
- **Jonathan Brockman (Spike)**
- **Jasmine Cameron**
- **Cassidy Shore**
- **Ryan Saltarelli (Salty)**
- **Kenzie Armstrong**
- **Matthew Stewart**
- **Connor Anderson**
- **Lisa Mayfield**
- **Alexandra Thompson**
- **Brett Sherbrooke**
- **Jennifer Wallace**
- **Nicole Vincent**

PROLOGUE

"Are you expecting the usual suspects tonight?" Spencer asked.

Lost in her thoughts, Maddie hadn't heard her brother come home. "Yeah, more or less."

About once a month, she invited friends over. Sometimes they just sat outside around the firepit, listening to music and snacking on whatever she'd whipped up. Other times, they played poker and then ventured outside, depending on the weather. No matter the game plan for the evening, the guest list always looked similar.

Tonight, she had everything set up inside for poker. However, she also had four cords of wood sitting near the firepit for when they moved the gathering outside, because the forecast called for a beautiful summer evening.

"Any idea if Connor is coming? It's about time I got even with him for cleaning me out during the last game."

After accepting a position at Lafayette Laboratory five months ago, Spencer had relocated back to Virginia and moved in with her until he found something of his own. To date, he'd joined all the gatherings she'd hosted. During the last poker game, Connor Anderson, a coworker of hers, had walked away with a decent amount of everyone's money.

"Becca bought tickets for a concert, so Connor won't be here," Maddie answered, her eyes glued to the meat thermometer she'd stuck in a chicken wing.

It might be rude not to even glance in her brother's direction, but she didn't care right now. Somehow, her older brother always knew when she was lying or stretching the truth. And she wasn't being completely honest now. While Connor wasn't coming tonight, it wasn't because his girlfriend had bought tickets to a concert. Instead, it was because she hadn't invited him or any other coworker except one—something she'd never done.

If she told Spencer the truth, he'd start asking other questions. The guy was noisier than her great-aunt Giorgia, and that was saying something. The woman knew everyone's business within a ten-mile radius of her home. Even as a child, Spencer had needed to know everything, even if it didn't pertain to him. So if Spencer learned she'd only invited one coworker, he'd interrogate her until the guests arrived. Then, if he felt she was still withholding info, he'd start again when everyone left. She already had enough on her mind without adding her older brother's questions to the mix.

"Figures." Opening the refrigerator, Spencer grabbed a bottle of flavored water. "Do you want anything?"

After removing the first two trays of buffalo wings from the oven, she set the baking sheets on the counter and put the next two in. A fan favorite among her friends, she made her special buffalo wings recipe whenever she had friends over. She'd heard about it for weeks the one time she'd made jalapeño poppers instead.

"I'm good for now, thanks," Maddie answered as she set the oven timer.

Although they were still too hot to eat, in her opinion,

Spencer grabbed a wing and bit into it. "Have I told you how much I love living with you? Maybe I won't move out."

"Please, we both know the only reason you love it here is because you get to eat whatever I cook."

"That is a nice perk. And since we're talking about food, did you make more salsa? We're all out."

That was another recipe she'd created, and Maddie always had some on hand. Or at least almost always. Since Spencer moved in, Maddie often found it gone whenever she wanted some. That had been the case last night. She'd been all set to watch the movie version of Elizabeth Gaskell's novel, *North and South*, while snacking on tortilla chips and salsa. Unfortunately, there hadn't been any salsa in the refrigerator, and she'd settled for popcorn instead.

"And whose fault is that?"

"Yours," Spencer said before taking another bite of his chicken wing.

"Mine? How did you reach that conclusion?"

"If it didn't taste so good, I wouldn't eat it. And since you came up with the recipe, it's your fault."

Some conversations weren't worth continuing. This was one of those. "Whatever you say."

The doorbell put a temporary halt to their conversation. "Make yourself useful and put the chips in bowls."

"All of them?"

She'd bought four different kinds. "Yes."

Crossing the living room, Maddie opened the front door. "Hey, Declan. All alone tonight?"

Declan Morris lived in the house next door, and they'd become friends the day she moved into the neighborhood. The guy had a great personality and a sense of humor that left her laughing until she cried. And for a while, she'd thought about asking him out. But before she could, he'd introduced her to Robert, his then fiancé, now husband.

"Robert hit traffic on the way home. He thinks he'll be here in about half an hour."

Maddie watched Jasmine get out of her car at the curb and close the door just as Keith, the only coworker she'd invited, pulled his motorcycle up behind her. Rather than walk toward the house, Jasmine headed in Keith's direction.

Big surprise.

Instead of doing what she wanted, which was stroll down to the sidewalk so she could hear their conversation, she gestured toward the casserole pan Declan held.

"What kind of dip did you go with tonight?" Like her, Declan loved experimenting in the kitchen. Almost every time he came over, he brought something new.

"Eggplant parmesan dip."

Don't look.

Despite her brain's message, her eyes had ideas of their own. She glanced in Keith and Jasmine's direction in time to see her friend swat Keith playfully on the arm and laugh at whatever he'd said.

Stepping back so Declan could enter, Maddie clenched her fists behind her back. "Sounds amazing."

It's going to be a long night.

AFTER FILLING A PLATE WITH FOOD, Keith sat down and hoped Maddie's friend Cassidy didn't go for the empty chair next to him when she came back outside. The woman hadn't left him alone since he arrived three hours ago. If it were just a matter of Cassidy never shutting up, he wouldn't mind as much. Sure, hearing her unusually high-pitched voice would be a pain in the ass, but he could tune anyone out, a useful skill to have growing up with two younger sisters. But it wasn't just a matter of Cassidy telling him her life story, starting at the age of five.

During the poker game, she had been practically sitting in his lap. He'd tried putting some space between them, but if he'd moved any farther to the left, he would've been sitting in Spencer's lap. He didn't know Spencer well, but Keith didn't think the guy would've appreciated that. Not that it helped anyway, because each time he shifted his chair away from Cassidy, the damn woman followed. Engaging in a game of follow-the-leader wasn't all she'd done either. She'd touched him every chance she got.

At first, it had been subtle. Each time Cassidy reached for her drink, her arm brushed against his, or when she shifted her position, her leg rubbed against his. If it had stopped at that, he'd chalk it up as a side effect of her sitting so close to him. But then she'd placed her hand on his thigh. And before he fully comprehended her intention, she'd slipped it higher and covered his crotch.

Seven months ago, he would've asked Cassidy back to his apartment when Maddie's little get-together ended. Hell, he might have suggested they leave then and there. No question about it, the woman was hot as hell. A full-time fitness instructor, she also competed in bikini bodybuilding shows. But not tonight.

Instead, he moved her hand away and wished Spike or Matt, two of his single coworkers, were there. Then maybe he could nudge Cassidy in their direction. Spike probably wouldn't have taken her home with him—the guy liked to know a woman well before sleeping with her—but he would have at least captured Cassidy's attention. On the other hand, Matt would've been escorting her out the door and to his car at the first sign she was interested. Unfortunately, Keith seemed to be on his own this evening. If any of his and Maddie's coworkers had planned to come, they would've been here hours ago.

Keith had been wondering about the lack of coworkers for much of the night. In the year and a half he'd worked with Maddie, or Mad Dog, as the other members of the Hostile Response Team—or HRT—called her, he'd attended a handful of poker games and several cookouts at her place. Whenever he did, at least a couple of team members also came. Tonight, other than him, the guest list consisted of Maddie's older brother, who was temporarily living with her, Maddie's neighbors, and her friends Cassidy and Jasmine.

While all their coworkers wouldn't have come, it seemed unlikely that everyone but him declined the invitation this evening. At the same time, it didn't make sense that Maddie would invite him and not everyone else. Keith considered the members of HRT to be more than coworkers or friends. He saw them as family. He'd never asked, but he knew everyone on the team felt the same way. That was just one of the reasons he'd hesitated to cross the line with Maddie. Getting involved with her could jeopardize not only his friendship and working relationship with her but also the rest of the team too. The second reason was a problem of his own fucking making.

Until a few months ago, he'd viewed her as Mad Dog Dempsey, a woman who spoke several languages, had once worked on an FBI SWAT team, and shot more accurately than him. And since she'd been just another teammate, he'd held nothing back if Maddie was around, so she knew a lot about his private life. And up until a few months ago, his personal life included casual hookups and no-strings-attached dating.

He'd stopped seeing her as a friend and coworker back in the spring. Now Maddie infiltrated his thoughts at least once a day. The worst, though, was on the weekends when he knew she might be off screwing some faceless dude a friend set her up with—not that he had any evidence she spent her weekends doing that. But like everyone else on the team, Maddie held very little back regarding her private life. So, Keith knew her friends were constantly setting her up with single men they knew. At least since he'd known her, though, Maddie never fell for any of them. Yeah, a few lucky SOBs got multiple dates, but none ever had their phone number stay in Maddie's contact list for more than a couple of months. Most didn't even get added to it.

And every time those damn thoughts invaded his mind, Keith wished he'd kept his big trap shut more often when she'd been around rather than talk about whoever he'd left Shooter's Pub with Saturday night—something he hadn't done in months. Not only hadn't he left the pub or any other bar with a woman, but he'd lived like a monk all summer, a fact Salty and Spike loved to bust his balls about every chance they got. At least they were the only ones, though.

He shared a lot with his friends, but he'd kept his feelings for Maddie to himself, or at least he'd tried. Unfortunately, months ago, he'd met up with Salty and Spike on a Saturday night when he knew Maddie had a date with some guy named George who worked with Maddie's friend Jasmine. Hoping they'd help chase away the X-rated visions of what Maddie and her date were up to, he'd had one too many beers. The drinks hadn't done a damn thing about his imagination. But they had caused him to open his big mouth and spill his guts. The following day, he woke on Spike's sofa with a raging headache. Thankfully, the only time Salty or Spike gave him a hard time about his lack of a sex life and the reason behind it was when none of the other team members were around. As much as it drove him crazy, he couldn't fault either of them. Salty was no longer single, but if Spike found himself in a similar position tomorrow, Keith would do precisely the same thing to him. Unfortunately, that would never happen because Spike, unlike him, was smart enough never to find himself in such a situation.

Keith's eyes remained focused on the back door as Maddie and Cassidy exited the house, clearly engrossed in a conversation.

What the hell are they talking about?

Was Cassidy setting Maddie up on a date for this weekend? Tomorrow night, instead of sitting outside with her friends, would Maddie be naked in bed with some bodybuilder Cassidy knew named Bill?

An image of a guy with biceps the size of Keith's thighs

lying on Maddie's bed while she moved her lips down his chest formed, and he clenched his jaw, sending pain through his cheek.

"Hey, you look upset. Is everything okay, Keith?" Jasmine asked, sitting down next to him.

Keith looked away from Maddie and Cassidy, but unfortunately, the bedroom scene continued to play out in his head. Sometimes his imagination was too damn good.

"Yeah, I just thought of something I need to do at work on Monday."

"Work is one thing I do not want to think about tonight. I've only been back two weeks, and I'm already counting the days until I'm back in Puerto Rico."

Some days were better than others, but he could honestly say he loved his job. Of course, it probably helped that he liked everyone he worked with, which wasn't the case for a lot of people.

"I've never been there, but my sister Kristen and her husband went last year. She said it was amazing. They want to go back next year, but they promised my niece a trip to Florida over February's school break," Keith said

"She's right. I go there at least twice a year. If my family didn't all live in Virginia and I knew I could find a job, I'd move there in a heartbeat. You need to visit." Leaning toward him, Jasmine placed her hand on his arm. "Don't get me wrong, the beaches around here are nice, but they're nothing like the ones there. The water is crystal clear, and the weather is perfect. I think I spent almost my whole vacation on a lounge chair in my bikini. The only place with equally nice weather is Hawaii. But the flight there is just too darn long."

"Both are on my bucket list of places to visit someday."

Thanks to his time in the army, he'd seen more of the world than many people. Most of those places, though, weren't locations people vacationed in.

"I think you made the right call," Maddie said to Cassidy.

At the sound of Maddie's voice, Keith looked away from

Jasmine and watched as Maddie and Cassidy stopped near chairs on the other side of the firepit. Although Maddie sat down, Cassidy remained standing as they continued their conversation.

Please park your ass over there.

He wasn't up for a repeat performance of keep-away with Cassidy right now.

"I don't know what Maddie does to them, but no one makes better buffalo wings," Declan, Maddie's neighbor, said as he stopped at the table near Keith long enough to refill his plate. Once finished, Declan made himself at home in the empty chair next to Keith, and he had never in his life been so happy to have a dude sitting next to him instead of a beautiful woman.

"Maddie's buffalo wings are good," Jasmine commented, "but there's a bar in Puerto Rico called Mojito that serves some that are like nothing I've tasted anywhere. And I make sure I stop in at least once when I'm there."

Jasmine slid her fingertips down his forearm. When she reached his wrist, she reversed her path. Keith remembered Maddie telling him her friend would flirt with anyone with a Y chromosome. Tonight, though, was the first time she'd turned her attention his way. He guessed it was because she'd arrived alone, whereas all the other times he'd seen her at Maddie's, she'd been with someone. Much like with Cassidy, he wouldn't have minded Jasmine's attention several months ago. But, unlike Cassidy, who would've fit in perfectly at the Playboy Mansion, Jasmine had more of a girl-next-door look, something that always turned him on. Maddie shared the same look, although in her case it was more of a girl-next-door who can kick your ass if she needs to.

"I even asked the manager for the recipe last time I was there, but he wouldn't give it to me," Jasmine said with a slight pout.

Keith reached for his drink, more to dislodge Jasmine's hand than because he was thirsty. "Yeah, a lot of restaurants won't give out recipes."

Next to him, Declan reached over and snagged the last wing off the platter without asking first if anyone wanted it. "Are there any more buffalo wings inside?"

Maddie paused in her conversation with Cassidy to answer. "Yeah, I'll go heat more."

"I can do it," Declan said after licking the sauce from his fingers. While the wings were out of this world, they were also messy.

Putting down her soda, Maddie stood. "You're a guest. I don't mind. Does anyone else need anything?" She glanced around the group, but her gaze seemed to linger on him longer than anyone else.

Did I imagine it?

Her brother held up his empty bottle in response to her question. "Another hard cider, if you remember."

Keith watched Maddie walk back into the house. He'd hoped to get her alone tonight so they could talk. About what, he had no damn clue, but talking seemed like a good way to gauge her feelings toward him. Now might be the only chance he got.

"You know, I could use another drink too." Keith stood, dislodging Jasmine's hand for a second time. "I'll be back."

But I just might find a different seat when I return.

When he entered the kitchen, Maddie stood with her back against the counter and her eyes closed.

"Hey, is everything okay?"

She opened her eyes as he closed the door behind him. "Yeah. Just getting a little tired. Some coffee might help." Pushing off the counter, she set her drink down. "Do you want anything?"

Yeah, you.

He didn't make a habit of lying, but he felt dumb telling her he'd followed her inside because he wanted to talk. "I came inside to see if you needed any help. But if you don't mind, I'll grab myself one of those." He pointed toward the hard cider she'd put down on the counter.

"Help yourself."

After opening the bottle, Keith watched her reach for something inside the cupboard. The action caused her T-shirt to ride up, exposing her lower back and tormenting him. His fingers itched to touch the bare skin, see if it was as smooth as it looked. And if he knew doing so wouldn't earn him a slap to the face, or worse, he would do it.

Dragging his eyes away from the tantalizing strip of skin, he searched for a safe topic. Maddie and her brother were close, so he figured he couldn't go wrong there. "How long is Spencer staying here?" If she'd already told him, he didn't remember.

"Spencer made an offer on a condo near Jasmine earlier this week, and the owners accepted it, so probably not too much longer."

Evidently, Maddie didn't find what she wanted because she moved her attention to a higher shelf, revealing more skin in the process. Before he did something stupid, and his imagination was full of stupid actions right now, Keith shoved his hands in his pockets and leaned against the counter.

Vacations were usually safe topics too, and she'd recently returned from a short one. "Did Cassidy and Jasmine go with you to Myrtle Beach last weekend?"

She'd told him it was a girls' weekend but not who she'd traveled with or what they'd done. Honestly, Keith wasn't sure he wanted to know what or who she'd done while down there, but asking about the trip gave him a reason to stick around.

"Only Cassidy did. She needed it. She just got out of a long relationship and needed some time to vent."

"You mean she needed a chance to man bash." He'd heard his two sisters do enough of that over the years, especially when a relationship turned sour.

Maddie shrugged. "Maybe a little." Grabbing a bag of coffee, she set it down next to the coffeepot and went back to searching the cupboard. "So, which one is going to be the lucky lady tonight? If you need help, I can distract one while you leave with the other."

"Thanks for the offer," he said, unable to keep the annoyance out of his voice. Maddie couldn't blame Cassidy's and Jasmine's behavior on him. He'd done nothing to encourage either woman tonight. And if he could tell them both to get lost without being rude, he would.

It might not matter, but Keith needed her to know he wasn't interested in either of her friends. "I know they're your friends, but part of the reason I came in here was to get away from them both."

Giving up her search, Maddie turned and faced him. "Are you feeling okay? Should I get the thermometer and check your temperature?"

Maddie looked so surprised, Keith couldn't contain his smile as he moved away from the counter and toward her. "I'm feeling fine, but I won't stop you if you want to play nurse."

"If you want a nurse, we should call Neil. He was a medic in the navy," she said, referring to another team member.

"I'm not interested in Neil either."

Grow a damn set already. Spike's recent recommendation echoed in his head.

Ignoring the possible repercussions, Keith stepped closer and put his hands on her shoulders. Then, when Maddie didn't move away or tell him to back off, he lowered his head toward hers, giving her plenty of time to pull away. And when she didn't do that or something worse, he brushed his lips against hers.

Rather than push him away—actually, Maddie would've given him a violent shove or a fist to the gut if she wanted him to stop—her arms went around his neck, and she leaned into him. He'd wanted to taste her for so long, and it took every ounce of self-control not to tease her lips apart and plunge inside like he'd done so many times in his dreams.

"Hey, Maddie, we're all out of salsa. Do we have any more?" Spencer asked from behind him.

At the sound of her brother's voice, Maddie pulled away so fast one would think a starting pistol had gone off and she was running the 100-meter dash.

Great situation awareness.

He hadn't even heard the door open. Of course, that wasn't a big deal, since he was standing in Maddie's kitchen. But when he was on an assignment, it could mean the difference between life and death.

Maddie didn't look at either of them as she headed for the stove. "There's a container in the refrigerator with more. Just take the whole thing outside."

After turning off the timer, she removed a tray of buffalo wings from the oven and transferred them to a platter in silence.

Spencer took his sweet time getting the salsa. Eventually, though, he left with it, as well as the hard cider he'd asked Maddie to bring out to him earlier.

Alone again, Maddie turned around, holding a platter piled high with wings. She looked both annoyed—hopefully Spencer was the cause of that emotion—and something bordering on confused. He didn't have to wonder about who or what had caused the second emotion.

"You're not interested in the two women outside letting you know they'd be more than willing to leave with you tonight, and then you kiss me. What's going on with you, Keith?"

"If your brother hadn't interrupted us, I'd still be kissing you." He hadn't answered her question, but he'd been honest with her.

"Keith?"

He thought the kiss would've told her what was going on with him. But, since it hadn't, he'd go with plan B. He removed the platter from her hands and set it down. He couldn't kiss her again with it between them.

He hated when people left you guessing as to the true meaning of their words. It might cause uncomfortable situations, sometimes even hostile ones, but he believed in straightforward, bullshit-free conversations. And by the time they left this kitchen, Maddie would know how he felt. Hopefully, he didn't kill their friendship in the process.

"Ever since I walked inside the house, I've wanted to kiss you."

When his words didn't earn him a kick toward the door, or worse, he put his hand on her shoulder and moved his thumb slowly back and forth across her clavicle. Her skin felt even better against his than he'd imagined.

"Do you have plans for tomorrow?"

"No, not really."

"Good. Let's do something together." He should give her a chance to answer. But he'd already exhausted whatever self-control he had and couldn't keep himself from kissing her again. "Whatever you want to do, we'll do," he said after his first pass over her lips. He didn't care as long as it didn't involve anyone but them.

"Okay."

He didn't give her a chance to say anything else.

KICKING OFF THE BLANKETS, Maddie rolled onto her back. For the past two hours, she'd been staring into the darkness, unable to fall asleep. She could blame that all on one person, too. Keith Wallace.

Technically, it wasn't the first time since they'd met that he had affected her sleep. At least a couple of times a month, she woke up from an erotic dream starring him and then lay awake wishing he was there so they could act it out.

She'd spent her adult life working in male-dominated fields, yet she'd never fantasized about a coworker until him. Precisely what it was about Keith, she couldn't put her finger on. True, he was handsome, but not big-screen-worthy like Spike. And there really was no other way to describe Spike. The guy should be starring in action films, not living in Virginia and working with her. Regardless, the day all six-feet-two inches of Keith walked into the team meeting room, he'd captured her attention, and he'd had it ever since.

Unfortunately.

Despite wanting to rip the guy's clothes off every time he entered whatever room Maddie was in, she'd initially treated him the same way she did the other guys on the team. Romantic relationships in the workplace often brought issues. Ones she wasn't sure any guy was worth, no matter how attracted to them she was. It hadn't taken long for Maddie to nix the idea of them ever being more than friends.

Although she went on a lot of dates, usually with men her friends set her up with, she didn't do one-night stands or leave bars with guys she'd just met. Unfortunately, the same couldn't be said about Keith. Like the other guys on the team, Keith wasn't shy when it came to talking about his sex life, so she knew it wasn't unusual for the guy to sleep with a woman he'd just met or take out a different woman every weekend. While she didn't need a man to get down on his knee and profess his undying love, she wanted someone who could commit to her for more than forty-eight hours—something Keith was incapable of doing.

Or at least she'd believed that until recently.

The day he'd picked her up at the airport, she'd accused him of having an aversion to relationships that might lead somewhere. Rather than come back with a response, something like he preferred his sex life to be a buffet where he could sample different women rather than a sit-down meal, Keith had informed her the only thing he had an aversion to was oysters. While it could've been just a sarcastic reply—the guy was known for them—something in his eyes said otherwise. Then again, whatever she saw or thought she saw could've been caused by the airport lighting.

Either way, the comment had bugged her all week. Although

she wasn't proud of it, she'd invited Keith but not the other members of HRT to her house, expecting Jasmine to let him know she was open to some adult fun tonight. And since Jasmine was single again—her most recent relationship had lasted all of two weeks before she gave him the boot—she would do that. The first time Jasmine had met Keith at a cookout, she'd commented that she'd do him in a heartbeat, although she'd been dating someone at the time. And when Jasmine came on to Keith, Maddie envisioned them leaving together.

What she hadn't expected was for Cassidy to flirt with him too. Well, maybe flirt was too mild a word. She'd known Cassidy for years, and she'd never seen her behave like she had tonight. Her friend had practically been sitting in Keith's lap during the poker game. Maddie chalked her unusual behavior up to it being her way of getting over the recent disastrous end to her engagement. And when she'd seen the attention Cassidy was giving Keith, she'd known he wouldn't turn down her offer. Cassidy was beyond gorgeous. Although she'd never admit it, Maddie was a little envious of her. Even on her best days, when Maddie put in the effort, she couldn't compete with Cassidy.

Instead of leaving with either woman, though, Keith had followed her into the kitchen and proceeded to show her how unskilled every guy she'd ever kissed was before asking her to spend the day with him tomorrow. Like an idiot, she'd allowed her body, rather than her brain, to decide for her. No longer subjected to Keith's lazy grin, the one she'd seen him use on other women and that guaranteed he never left a bar alone, her brain was reconsidering her answer.

The man never had trouble finding a weekend companion, so he wouldn't have turned to her if that was all he wanted. Not only that, but Keith also wouldn't risk their working relationship or friendship for a night or two of sex. Still, that didn't mean crossing out of the friend zone was a good idea. Once left, the friend zone was almost impossible to return to. And Maddie could easily see Keith deciding he preferred his casual hookups after a couple of weeks. Even if she was the one to end things, it might make working together uncomfortable. And not just for the two of them. The end of their relationship could create a sticky situation for the entire team.

Or we might end up growing old and gray together.

Keith had turned down not only Jasmine but Cassidy tonight, proving anything could happen.

ONE

Eight weeks later

"LOOKS like I'm not the only one with nothing to do tonight."

Maddie glanced away from the inside of her gym locker and toward the room's newest occupant. Actually, Lisa was the only other person in the locker room, which wasn't a big surprise, considering it was a Friday night. Most people had better things to do on a Friday night than go to the gym and run on a treadmill.

"Hey, Lisa. How's it going?"

"Could be better. Teddy canceled on me at the last minute tonight. We were supposed to go to Moonshiner's Bar, where his friend's band is performing, but his parents needed a ride home from the airport. Since I had nothing else to do, I decided to get in a workout. What's your excuse for being here?"

Although Elite Force Security's headquarters housed a state-of-the-art gym complete with a lap pool, Maddie belonged to one close to her house. While she loved the people she worked with—truthfully, her coworkers were more like family—sometimes she needed a break from the testosterone-filled gym and the rest of the team. Coming here once a week or so gave her that. It also gave her a chance to meet new people and make friends. Jasmine and Cassidy, two of her closest friends—well, closest nonwork friends—she'd met there not long after accepting the job with Elite Force three years ago. The fourth person in their little group, Kayleen, she'd met through the other two.

Lisa, though, she'd met a few weeks ago. Maddie had been less than half a mile into her run when Lisa hopped on the treadmill next to her. They'd finished at the same time, and then, on the walk back to the locker room, Lisa had started a conversation. Although Maddie wouldn't put Lisa in the same category as Jasmine or Cassidy, she considered her more than just an acquaintance. They'd even met up for dinner one night after leaving the gym.

"I haven't worked out all week and had some time to kill tonight," Maddie answered. How much time was anyone's guess. She hadn't heard from Keith, which meant he and Spike were still sitting inside a run-down apartment in an unsavory neighborhood, listening to Neil's wire in case he needed backup. But, of course, she couldn't tell Lisa that.

While everyone knew the forty-plus-year-old firm provided private security to anyone who could afford it, Elite Force did a hell of a lot more, especially the Hostile Response Team. The past summer alone, the team had tracked down a computer scientist who'd stolen top-secret technology, rescued a mom and her young daughter who were being held in Mexico against their will, and safely extracted Salty's girlfriend and her mom from a criminal bent on revenge.

Opening her locker, Lisa tossed her keys and sweatshirt inside before removing her water bottle from her duffel bag and setting it down on the bench. "Is your boyfriend working late again?"

They'd been together for roughly eight weeks, yet Maddie still found it difficult to associate the term "boyfriend" with

Keith. But she hadn't come up with a better word to describe him, either.

"Yep." After adding her wet towels to her bag, Maddie grabbed her boots and sat down.

"Speaking of boyfriends, were you and Keith at Murphy's Tavern on Monday night?"

Monday night, she'd just safely delivered Lady Haverston, President Sherbrooke's mother-in-law, and her granddaughter to their hotel when Keith called asking if she wanted to meet him and Connor at Murphy's for a late dinner and a few drinks.

"Yeah, I met him and a friend after work. You should've come over and said hello." Besides Keith and Connor, she had seen no one she recognized that night, but the place had been crowded.

"I wasn't positive it was you," Lisa answered with a slight shrug. "But damn, he's cute. Does he have any brothers?"

"Sorry, no. Just two younger sisters."

"What about the friend that was with you? The guy's like walking sex in jeans."

Well, Lisa wasn't wrong. "Connor has a girlfriend."

"That figures," Lisa said as she pulled her dark hair up. "So Keith is working late again. He seems to do that a lot. Doesn't it bother you?"

Maddie worked late and odd hours just as often as Keith, including over the past several weeks. Both went with the job. "No, not really."

"Really? I'd always wonder if he was at work or with someone else," Lisa said as she changed into a cropped workout T-shirt that read "Witness my Fitness."

Maddie had known both men and women who would screw around behind their significant other's back without a second thought. In fact, about three months ago, she'd caught Patrick, Cassidy's fiancé, with another woman. Talk about an awkward conversation with both parties. Patrick had even gone so far as to offer her money in exchange for not telling Cassidy. Not surprisingly, he was now Cassidy's ex-fiancé, hence the need for their girls-only weekend to Myrtle Beach two and half months ago.

"Keith wouldn't do that."

All his many faults aside, Keith valued honesty and loyalty, two words cheaters didn't know the meaning of. Even when he'd been taking a different woman out every weekend, he'd been upfront with them that he wasn't looking for anything long-term.

Shaking her head, Lisa sat down on the bench. "That's what I thought about my ex-husband. It turned out that when Ralph said he was working late, he was screwing his administrative assistant. Something similar happened to my cousin. Take it from me: you just never know what someone else is really doing when you're not with them."

In Maddie's opinion, it sounded like Lisa had some major trust issues, which didn't bode well for any future relationships. But maybe she would too, in Lisa's shoes. She'd had relationships end, but she'd never had a boyfriend cheat on her.

"What are you up to this weekend?" Maddie asked, as a way to change the subject. It was better to avoid discussing relationships with some people. Unfortunately, based on what Lisa just said, she was one of them.

"Nothing at the moment. You?"

"Keith and I haven't talked about it. Originally, I was supposed to work this weekend, but now I'm off until Monday morning."

For the past five weeks, her assignment had been to escort President Sherbrooke's mother-in-law and his niece, who were visiting from England, around. Not just around the immediate area, either. Since their arrival, they'd traveled to Manhattan, where the two women had done more shopping in a few days than Maddie did in a year before seeing a Broadway show. They'd also flown to California, and most recently, they'd spent two days on Martha's Vineyard. The two women were definitely making the most of their visit to the United States.

"Well, if you have nothing to do, call me. I want to check out that new winery on Chestnut Street, but I don't want to go alone. And you're the only one of my friends that drinks wine. Everyone else I know prefers either mixed drinks or beer."

Maddie didn't see herself having nothing to do this weekend, but she wasn't opposed to visiting the new winery if it happened. She'd been curious about it since it opened last month, and a place like that was more fun to visit with a friend.

"Will do," Maddie said as she slipped the straps of her duffel bag over her shoulder. "Have a nice weekend."

"You too."

Less than five minutes later, her favorite Metallica song erupted from Maddie's cell phone as she started her car. It didn't surprise her to see Keith's name on the screen. Knowing he wouldn't be able to answer the phone if she called him while he was doing surveillance, she'd sent him a text letting him know she was going to the gym after depositing Lady Haverston and her granddaughter, Violet, at the White House.

"Spike and I just left Ax's office, and I'm starving. Do you want to meet us at Shooter's, or are you already home?"

Located not far from Elite Force Security headquarters, the team regularly visited the sports pub. If it meant she didn't have to cook or, more importantly, put on something nicer than the jeans and T-shirt she wore, she'd meet him anywhere for dinner. Over the past several weeks, she'd eaten at enough expensive restaurants that wouldn't let you in the door wearing jeans to last her a lifetime.

Maddie shifted her car into reverse. "Just leaving the gym now. I'll see you in a few."

The scent of burgers, beer, and french fries greeted Maddie when she walked inside. Despite the joint's run-down appearance, the popular sports pub had a steady stream of regular customers every day of the week, many of them military men and women from the nearby base. Like most Friday nights, there wasn't an empty seat in the place. Customers occupied all the stools at the bar, and both pool tables were in use.

She spotted Keith and Spike seated near the far wall, each with a beer in front of them. Candy, a pretty brunette wearing a sprayed-on Shooter's T-shirt and a short skirt, reached their table just as Maddie did. The waitress had worked there at least as long as Maddie had been coming to the restaurant and regularly flirted with male customers. Based on what she'd heard, it wasn't uncommon for the waitress to go home with a guy after her shift ended. She didn't know about Keith, and she didn't intend to ask, but Maddie knew Connor had taken the waitress home with him on more than one occasion before his girlfriend, Becca, entered his life.

"Here are your nachos," Candy said as she placed an overflowing plate on the table. One thing you could say about the pub was they didn't skimp on their orders.

Slipping into the booth next to Keith, Maddie reached for a menu, although honestly, she didn't need one. In all the time she'd been coming in, the pub had never changed the menu, and she'd probably tried everything they served at least once.

"Hey, Maddie. I haven't seen you in a while." Like the other longtime employees, Candy seemed to know the names of all the regulars.

Maddie guessed the last time she'd stopped in was last month. "I've had to do some traveling for work."

"Well, it's good to see you," Candy said, as she clasped her hands behind her back. "Do you all know what you want, or should I come back?"

"Can you come back? We're waiting for one more," Spike answered.

"You've got it. Just wave me down when you're ready." Then, turning on her heel, the woman sauntered toward another table, undoubtedly drawing the attention of several other customers.

Although Maddie hadn't sent her coworkers a memo letting them know she and Keith were together, they all knew. Regardless, she tried not to act any differently around Keith when they were with anyone from work. Unfortunately, that meant she had to keep her hands and lips to herself, even though it was the opposite of what she wanted to do right now.

Under the table, Keith gently squeezed her thigh. "Is the countess all tucked in for the night?"

If someone overheard Keith's comment, they might assume he used the term "countess" in a derogatory manner because the woman was a stuck-up, pain-in-the-ass socialite. They'd be wrong, though, because President Sherbrooke's mother-in-law was married to an earl, making her an actual countess—a fact that had initially made her cringe when she got the assignment.

While Lady Haverston was the first member of the nobility Elite Force had assigned to her, she'd worked for many of the firm's ultra-wealthy clients. Most were obnoxious individuals who thought their farts didn't stink. While President Sherbrooke's mother-in-law and his niece might feel the same way, they at least didn't act like it. In fact, the woman reminded Maddie of the grandmother in the *Princess Diaries* movies that her cousin's daughter was currently obsessed with. She'd watched it over and over the weekend Maddie had babysat her.

"More like for the next two days. Lady Haverston's grandson and his family flew in from New York tonight, and her granddaughter and her family are arriving tomorrow. She has no plans to leave the White House, so I've got the weekend off."

Keith squeezed her thigh again before slowly moving his hand higher. Between work and the brief trip Keith had taken up to see his family in Rhode Island, they had only spent three consecutive days together a handful of times since they moved out of the friend zone.

"Who are we waiting for?" She gestured toward the empty seat next to Spike as she debated whether she should do something about Keith's wandering hand and risk drawing Spike's attention or leave it be.

"Salty. Kenzie is working late at the clinic tonight. The poor guy can't function alone anymore," Spike answered.

Unlike everyone else who'd met after coming to work for Elite Force Security, Spike and Ryan Saltarelli, aka Salty, had grown up together in New Hampshire. Spike had even been the one to give Salty's name to the firm's director.

Reaching under the table, she wrapped her hand around Keith's before it got any further, since he clearly didn't plan to stop. "Someone sounds a little jealous, my friend."

"Of him?" Spike asked, gesturing toward Salty as he joined them. "What the hell is there to be jealous about? I mean, look at the guy. I think you've been spending too much time in museums lately, Mad Dog."

Keith no longer used the nickname the team had given her, but the other members still did. And that was fine with her because it told her they accepted her as part of the group despite being one of only two women on the HRT.

"A lot, my friend. Starting with the fact I never sleep alone," Salty said, grabbing a nacho off the platter and biting into it.

"Maddie, you might be on to something. Spike has been cranky lately," Keith said as he tried to free his hand from hers. "He must not be getting any. Maybe you should set him up with one of your friends."

Any of her friends would happily go out with Spike. A few, though, she'd never set him up with. "Kayleen is out. She and Hunter are practically engaged. But you and Cassidy would make a cute couple."

More like a jaw-droppingly beautiful couple, but she saw no need to tell Spike how gorgeous he was. Unless the guy didn't own a mirror, he already knew it. "Or maybe Sierra. She's not seeing anyone."

"Hey, what about Jasmine? Isn't she single again?" Keith successfully freed his hand from hers and turned the tables on her by trapping her hand on his thigh.

Jasmine was one of those friends she'd never set up with Spike. The woman went through men like most people went through underwear.

"Thanks, but no thanks," Spike answered. "I can find my own dates."

"Sure, you can. That's why you—" Salty began but stopped when Candy appeared at their table again.

Sometimes she enjoyed giving her friends a hard time. Tonight wasn't one of them. So, as soon as Candy left to put in their dinner orders, Maddie spoke before Salty could finish his comment. One that was sure to get a response from their single coworker. "So, Spike, has your sister decided what schools she's going to apply to?"

Weeks ago, Spike's much younger sister Audrey had toured several universities in the DC area. Spike's parents hoped she'd attend a school in New Hampshire, so they'd be close by in case she needed them. If she didn't, though, Spike, his parents, and even Salty, who considered Audrey a younger sister, hoped she'd attend some place around there, so Spike and Salty would be nearby if she needed them.

"Mad Dog with the save," Salty said as he helped himself to more nachos.

Well, that had been her goal.

"Georgetown is at the top of her list, followed by Providence College and UNH."

"Weren't Tulane and USC her top two?" Salty asked.

"Audrey decided she didn't want to be that far from family," Spike replied. "She decided not to apply to either. Thank God. Other than Georgetown, all the schools she's applying to now are in New England."

"Your parents must be happy," Maddie said.

She'd attended the University of Virginia. Although it'd been too far to commute, she'd been within a couple of hours' drive from her parents, unlike Spencer, who'd gone to college in Colorado.

"They're not the only ones," Spike said.

Maybe it was because they were much closer in age, but

neither Spencer nor Tucker had ever been overprotective older brothers the way Spike clearly was.

At the sound of the familiar guitar riff Keith used for incoming text messages, he released her hand and pulled out his phone. Whoever the message was from, he typed a quick response, and then he shoved it back into his pocket as he exchanged a look she couldn't decipher with Spike.

"Another one of those political messages asking for a donation?" Spike asked as he raised his beer toward his mouth.

The presidential election was about a year away, but campaigning was already well underway—not that it would help any of the candidates much, in her opinion. No matter how much money his opponents threw into their campaigns or how many messages they sent out, they'd never beat President Sherbrooke next year. He was simply too popular with the American public.

"I got one of those today." She'd deleted it without even reading the politician's whole spiel about why she should hand over some of her hard-earned money to help someone she'd never met. And probably someone she disagreed with.

Keith shook his head. "No, it was a message from my sister, Jen. I'll call her later."

NINETY MINUTES LATER, Keith grabbed the silent cell phone he'd tossed on the passenger seat as he opened his truck door and hoped the device remained that way.

When he'd heard the familiar tone while at Shooter's, he'd silently sworn and wished he could ignore the damn thing. But he'd known if he did that, it would only bring more attention to the fact he'd received a message, because he never ignored his phone. Everyone, including Maddie, knew it, because they were the same way. They had to be. One never knew when Ax, their team leader, might need them for an unplanned assignment. Unlike some women he'd dated, Maddie wasn't the type to question him every time he got a call or a text. Still, he hadn't wanted to draw attention to his phone just in case the message was anything like the ones he'd gotten last night and then earlier today.

For the third night in a row, he'd been alone for the evening, and he'd fallen asleep watching the baseball game. And when the guitar riff woke him up, Keith expected the text to be from either Maddie, who'd spent her evening at the National Theater with Lady Haverston and her granddaughter, or one of the guys.

It hadn't been from either.

Instead, the message read like a sex scene from an erotic novel… or how he imagined sex scenes in erotic stories would be. He wasn't much of a reader, and when he picked up a book, they tended to be historical nonfiction ones, not cheesy romances.

After sending back a "sorry you have the wrong number" text, he'd deleted the message, expecting that to be the end of it. But he got a similar one tonight as he followed Spike into the elevator after their debrief with Ax. Like last night, no phone number appeared with the text, telling him whoever sent it was using a messaging app. Unlike the previous night's, though, this time, the sender started with "Hi Keith" before detailing all the ways she wanted him to take her. So, either the messages were intended for another guy named Keith with a similar phone number, or he knew the sender and the texts were for him. He didn't need someone with a doctorate in statistics to tell him which was more likely. Last year at this time, he would've found the messages entertaining. He might have even suggested to whoever was sending them that they get together and act them out.

Now he found them to be a major pain in the ass. One that could torpedo his relationship with Maddie if she saw them and jumped to the wrong conclusion. He liked to think she trusted him, but he did have a shitty track record in the relationship department. And even though he trusted Maddie, if she'd been the one receiving the explicit messages and he saw them, he'd be pissed off.

Although they'd left the pub at the same time, thanks to the grandpa in front of him who didn't know you were supposed to speed up at a yellow light rather than stop at it, he'd hit the red light at the intersection of Maple and Grove—something no one ever wanted to do. The timing of the stupid thing was all screwed up, and it took an eternity for it to change from red to green.

Maddie opened the front door before he knocked. He didn't know how much sooner she'd gotten home, but she'd already changed into PJ shorts and a T-shirt featuring Oscar the Grouch. He'd find the outfit the farthest thing from being sexy on anyone else. But, on Maddie, it had him hoping they had enough condoms to get through the night, because he didn't feel like making a midnight trip to the store.

Following her lead, he kept his hands to himself when they were around their friends. Or at least he tried. Sometimes, like earlier tonight, he couldn't resist, but unless Spike or Salty had X-ray vision, they couldn't see where he'd had his hand under the table.

But no one was around now.

He didn't bother with a verbal greeting. Closing the door behind him, Keith covered her lips with his and pulled her against him. Without any encouragement, she parted her lips and leaned into him.

Soon kissing her was no longer enough. Sliding his hands under her T-shirt, he cupped her breast and moved his mouth to her neck.

"All day, I've been thinking about this." Slowly, he rubbed his thumb across her nipple, his body tightening a little more with each pass.

Yanking his shirt free of his waistband, Maddie placed her palms on his bare skin, sending Keith's current state of arousal from a six to a nine. "I thought you were monitoring Neil's wire." Her fingertips slowly traveled up his spine and then reversed course.

"It's called multitasking." Before moving his attention to her other breast, Keith gently pinched her nipple, and she groaned. "Don't you ever think of this while you're walking through museums and looking at paintings?"

"Nope."

Keith didn't believe her. "Not even when you're sitting through those plays?" He treated her left breast to the same treatment and was rewarded with another groan of pleasure.

Maddie shook her head as her hands moved from his back to his belt buckle. "There is only one time I think about this." She ran her palm down the length of him before going back to undo his belt. "When I'm alone at night and I have Mr. Big to do what you're not there to."

He could handle anything, but an image of Maddie pleasuring herself was almost enough to do him in.

With his belt out of the way, she slipped the button free on his jeans and eased the zipper down. "In case you were wondering, I thought about this last night when I got home from the theater." Shrugging, she met his eyes. "And, unfortunately, you weren't here."

Slamming his lips down on hers, Keith ran his fingertips down her back and under the waistband of her shorts. When his hands landed on bare skin instead of the soft cotton underwear he expected, what little self-control he had left vaporized. Somehow, he managed to get a condom from his wallet and put it on. Then, backing Maddie up against the door, Keith picked her up, and she wrapped her legs around his waist as he joined their bodies.

ON HIS SIXTEENTH BIRTHDAY, Keith had had sex for the first time. It'd been his birthday present from Melinda Percy, his girlfriend at the time. Her parents had gone on vacation and left

Melinda at home with her twenty-one-year-old sister, Leigh. Leigh, the loving older sister that she was, had bought them a six-pack of beer and then spent the night at her boyfriend's apartment, leaving them alone in the house.

Since Melinda, he'd slept with his fair share of women and enjoyed every second of it. But none of those experiences compared to sex with Maddie. It was as if he'd been playing in the minor league for the past eighteen years and was finally in the majors.

Rolling onto his side, Keith propped himself up on his elbow. After their quickie against the front door, they'd retreated down the hall to her bedroom, where they'd taken things at a much slower pace.

"You named your dildo?" he asked, her comment from earlier suddenly popping into his head.

"It's a vibrator," she replied without opening her eyes.

Like there's much of a difference.

"Okay, I'll rephrase. You named your vibrator?"

Maddie turned her head so she faced him and met his eyes. "Do you think I would do that?"

"Hey, you're the one who referred to it as 'Mr. Big,' not me."

"That's the name on the box it came in. But the name describes it well."

"Really?"

Maddie's lips curved into a smile as she nodded. "Don't worry, though, I much prefer you."

"Good to know I outperform a vibrator."

Her smile grew wider, and she patted him on the shoulder. "Hey, just be glad you're good at something."

"You really know how to boost a guy's ego," he said, pressing his lips against her forehead. "And just so you know, I'm a decent guitar player. Next time you come over, I'll prove it to you."

He'd never be in the same category as Eddie Van Halen or

Jimi Hendrix, but thanks to all the hours of practice he'd put in over the years, Keith was a damn good player.

The guitar riff he used for texts, one by his favorite musician, went off, bringing to mind the two unwanted messages he'd recently received. "I'm going to pretend I didn't hear that because I'd have to get out of bed to answer, and I'm too comfortable."

"It might be Ax."

"Or it's a stupid political survey asking me who I plan to vote for next year." From inside his jeans pocket, the tone sounded again.

Pushing off the sheets, Maddie sat up. "Because I like you and I don't want you to end up on Ax's bad side if it is him, I'll grab it for you. I'm getting up anyway to get something to drink."

Hell no.

He didn't want Maddie anywhere near his phone in case his mystery messenger had struck again.

"It's probably Jen. I told her I'd get back to her after talking to you." Standing up, Keith crossed the room and retrieved the jeans he'd left near the bedroom door.

Still naked, Maddie stopped next to him. "Do you want anything while I'm up?"

"Whatever you're having."

"Be right back."

Keith watched Maddie walk out of the room. One thing he'd learned about her over the past eight weeks was that she was just as comfortable walking around the house naked as she was fully dressed. And when they were either here or at his apartment, he got her naked as often as he could.

Neither Jen's nor Ax's name greeted him when he looked at the screen. Instead, he found a text from Colby Windsor, one of the few friends from high school he still communicated with. He hadn't heard from the guy in three or four weeks. It'd been even longer since he last saw him. Friends throughout high school, they'd both been on the football and wrestling teams. Then, during their freshman and sophomore years at URI, they'd shared a dorm room before moving to an off-campus apartment for their final two years of college. Keith had hoped to meet up with him the weekend he'd gone up to see his family, but Colby had been on vacation.

Keith read the text a second time. As far as he'd known, the guy had only recently gotten involved with someone. Yet now Colby was engaged to someone named Amari, and he wanted Keith to be the best man at his wedding.

He was still replying to his friend's surprising text when Maddie returned and handed him a root beer. Rather than join him in bed again, she grabbed an oversized T-shirt from a drawer and pulled it on, much to his disappointment.

"Was it Jen again?" she asked as her head emerged from the top of the shirt.

He set the device down when another text didn't appear on the phone. "No, Colby. We went to school together."

"Is he the one you hoped to see when you were in Rhode Island a few weeks ago?"

Maddie had the memory of an elephant and didn't forget anything. "Yeah. He asked me to be his best man."

"You don't sound thrilled about that. Is planning a bachelor party too much responsibility for you? If it is, I'm willing to help you."

"You're hilarious." Keith took a swig from the soda can. "Believe me, no one throws a better bachelor party than me. But he's only been dating this person for three or four months, and now he's getting married in a week."

"My parents were only together for three and a half months before they got married in Vegas, and their fortieth anniversary is in March. So it might work out for him."

"Did an Elvis impersonator perform your parents' ceremony?"

"No, it was one of those drive-through weddings." Nothing

about Maddie's expression hinted at whether or not she was serious. "They didn't even have to get out of the car."

"Really?"

Rolling her eyes, Maddie readjusted the pillow behind her before leaning back. "They got married in a chapel by a justice of the peace who wore a suit and tie. There were six guests there."

"Sounds kind of nice, actually."

When his sister Kristen got married, they'd had close to a hundred guests. And if his sister Jen and her boyfriend, Brett, who happened to be a longtime friend of his from the army, ever found themselves at the altar, the guest list would be close to three times as many, considering the family Brett belonged to. But, honestly, he saw no need to have that many people on hand for something so personal.

"I second that. When my brother Tucker got married, it was one of those over-the-top affairs. My sister-in-law even had two different wedding dresses, one for the ceremony and another for the reception. I adore Brittany, but let's just say money has never been an issue for her family, and her parents spoil her even now."

Although Maddie's parents and three siblings lived in Virginia, he'd never met her eldest brother, Tucker, or her younger sister, Autumn. But, assuming he didn't accidentally do something to fuck up their relationship, he saw that changing in the near future.

"Each to their own, I guess." Maddie shrugged before taking a drink. "Where is your friend getting married?"

"Up in Maine."

"Maine?"

It might not be Hawaii, but the state had a lot to offer, including a gorgeous coastline and terrific skiing. "What's wrong with Maine?"

"Nothing. But I thought he still lived in Rhode Island, so I expected you to say Newport or maybe Providence."

"He does live there, but only because the company he works for is located in Warwick. He goes up to Maine as often as possible and uses his grandparents' cottage. That's probably why he's getting married up there. Anyway, how do you feel about coming with me?" If Maddie came with him, it'd be the first time he attended a wedding with a date. "If we fly into Providence instead of Boston or Manchester, we can visit my parents before we drive up to Maine."

Introducing Maddie to his parents would be another in what was becoming a long list of firsts.

"Sure. Lady Haverston and Violet should be back on the other side of the Atlantic Ocean by then."

"Should? I thought they were leaving on the twentieth."

"As far as I know, they still are. But I overheard Violet asking her grandmother if they could spend another week here the other night. I didn't hear Lady Haverston answer."

It must be nice to not only go on vacation for six weeks but then be able to extend it an extra week if you wanted. The longest vacation he'd ever gone on had been for ten days.

"Since I've heard nothing from Ax yet, I'm guessing they're still leaving on the twentieth, so let's plan on me coming with you. Hopefully, your mom will have some nice embarrassing pictures of you to show me when we visit."

He didn't think Mom would pull out the family photo albums and embarrass the hell out of him, but a polite request asking her not to might not be a bad idea.

"Maybe we should stop and visit Kristen and Jen while we're in the area. As younger sisters, I'm sure they'd be happy to tell me some interesting stories about you."

Maddie's comment reminded Keith that he still needed to let Jen know if they could get together this weekend. "You might not need to wait even that long. A buddy Brett went to West Point with is getting married tomorrow, so he and Jen arrived in DC tonight. My sister wants to meet you before they go home."

"Your sister said she wants to meet me?" Maddie crossed her arms and gave him an I'm-not-buying-that expression.

He could read between the lines. "Her exact words were more like, 'let's get together.' But it's what she meant. I know my sister. Jen saw me a few weeks ago, so she didn't ask because she misses me and can't wait until Thanksgiving to see me again. So, what do you say?"

"Hey, I've subjected you to my brother Spencer enough times that meeting Jen is the least I can do."

TWO

THREE HOURS AFTER LEAVING THE GYM, HOURS THAT HAD BEEN possibly the longest of her life, Lisa turned onto Hearth Stone Road. After talking to Maddie in the locker room, rather than jump on a treadmill and run two miles before doing her upper-body workout, as she'd planned to do tonight, Lisa had wanted to drive to 14 Artemis Way and wait for Keith to come home. Or rather, wait for Keith and see whether he spent the night alone or not. But just because you wanted to do something didn't mean you should.

So instead, she forced herself upstairs to the cardio section of the gym and hoped some exercise would improve her mood and prevent her from doing something stupid. To date, all Lisa's encounters with the dumb bitch had left her madder than a wet hen, as her grandmother loved to say, and tonight's hadn't been any different—a fact she found somewhat unfortunate, because if they'd met under other circumstances, they might have eventually become close friends, something Lisa believed you could never have too many of in your life. Unfortunately, they hadn't.

Although Maddie didn't know it, she stood between Lisa and her soul mate.

About two months ago, when she first spotted Maddie and

Keith together in the parking lot at his apartment building, she assured herself it wouldn't last. Long before Keith ever said hello to her, Lisa had seen Keith come into Murphy's Tavern with a string of different women. And when they'd first started spending time together, he'd told her upfront he wasn't interested in anything long-term.

Despite his words, she'd known better.

Two people couldn't be as connected as they were and not realize it. But, like many people, Keith just wasn't ready to admit it. He'd ended things back in the spring for that reason rather than the excuse he'd given her. But eventually, Keith would realize he'd made a mistake and come knocking on her door. When he did, she'd take him back, no questions asked, because everyone made mistakes. And at the end of the day, they belonged together.

Soul mate or not, Lisa's patience had taken a hit about a week later when she saw the same chick enter Keith's building. Since the woman was alone, she gave Keith the benefit of the doubt and assumed the woman also lived in the building and was coming home, not visiting Keith. But not long after the woman entered the complex, Keith and who she now knew was Maddie Dempsey appeared on his balcony. Unable to do anything else, she'd spent the night in her car watching the complex's front door. Thankfully, the complex contained more than a hundred units, so an additional vehicle in the lot had gone unnoticed. And when the bitch didn't leave until the following morning, Lisa knew it was time to take control of the situation. Somehow, she had to come between them and help Keith reach the conclusion they belonged together, sooner rather than later.

Lisa's first instinct had been to knock on Keith's door and announce she was pregnant, ideally while his newest friend was there. However, she'd dismissed the idea almost immediately, because while it might temporarily strain his and the brunette's relationship, she'd be back to square one as soon as Keith learned the truth.

Once the knee-jerk reaction passed, Lisa realized the best way to get the woman out of the picture was to either make it appear as if Keith was cheating on her, get him actually to do it, or, as an absolute last resort, have the unknown woman permanently disappear.

Her first task had been determining the brunette's identity. On her first attempt to get more information, she'd spent almost three hours sitting outside Keith's apartment building, waiting for him to leave and lead her to the unknown woman's home. When he finally headed out, she'd discovered it was far more difficult to follow someone without making it look like you were following them than she'd anticipated. Once during the ride, she'd even lost him and had to guess whether he'd gone left or right at the intersection. Even worse, though, the bowling alley turned out to be his destination. While he'd possibly agreed to meet the brunette there, the location provided no clues to the woman's identity. Afraid of being seen by Keith, Lisa hadn't stuck around to see if he went anywhere else later.

She'd gone into attempt number two with the same plan, to wait for Keith to leave home and follow him to hopefully his girlfriend's house this time. An hour into her wait, the very woman she wanted more information about left the complex instead. Unlike during her previous attempt, Lisa managed to keep the vehicle in sight until the driver pulled into the garage at a single-family house on Hearth Stone Road. A quick search on the town assessor's database brought up the current owner's name, when she'd purchased the home, and even how much she'd paid for it.

Since Maddie lived on a street full of single-family homes rather than in a large apartment complex, Lisa couldn't wait outside for long periods and then follow her when she left. But, at the same time, she needed a way to meet and hopefully develop a friendship with her. So, at a loss of how to learn Maddie's daily routine without being seen, Lisa called a private investigating firm, the same one her cousin had used to gather all the proof she needed when her husband was cheating on her.

Carla Holmes, the investigator she met with, hadn't batted an eye when Lisa provided her with a similar story her cousin used when she'd hired the firm. The firm also hadn't questioned why she wanted to pay them in cash rather than via a credit card. But, more importantly, within ten days, Carla had a report and photos detailing not only the places Maddie visited but also how often per week and around what times she went and if she was alone.

Once she had the info, she'd joined Maddie's gym and stopped there around the exact times the investigator had seen her there. She spotted Maddie using a treadmill in the cardio section during her third visit and jumped on the one next to her. Outgoing by nature, she could strike up a conversation with anyone. So when Maddie finished her run, she'd done the same and commented to her about how she preferred running outside but it was too damn hot out as they walked back to the locker room. She'd been slowly cultivating their friendship ever since. And while Keith had come up during their conversations, Lisa avoided mentioning him.

Tonight, when she saw Maddie, it seemed like the right time to put a little bug in her ear by sharing the story of Ralph and his administrative assistant… with one slight change. Ralph had been her cousin's two-timing husband, not hers.

While she'd love it if a single story convinced Maddie Keith was doing something other than working, she knew better. And that was why she'd started sending text messages to Keith this week. After all, she didn't know any women who didn't check their boyfriend's text messages whenever they got the chance. She certainly always did. Some women went even further than that. Rachel, her sister, hacked into the email accounts of her boyfriends and read what they wrote.

"Please don't be together," Lisa said as she slowly made her way down the street toward Maddie's house.

She'd made the same statement when she drove by Keith's

apartment after initially leaving the gym. At least at the time, neither his truck nor Maddie's car had been in the parking lot, which meant Keith could be anywhere, including at work. Maddie had said he was working late, and she had no reason to lie about that. Still, she'd taken a drive over to Murphy's Tavern, an Irish pub close to her house and where they'd met. Unfortunately, there was no sign of him there or at Shooter's, another place he liked to visit. But if he had been at either and without any of his usual friends, guys that must be friendly with Maddie because she'd seen them all together at the sports pub, she would've done everything she could to get him back to her place. And after they spent the night together, Keith would realize the mistake he'd made and again be hers.

Lisa jerked the steering wheel to the right and slammed on the brakes three-quarters of the way down the street. "Fuck."

Keith's dark green truck sat in Maddie's driveway, silently taunting her, reminding her he was at another woman's house. Maybe even right this minute he was bringing another woman to orgasm.

He shouldn't be in that house. They should be together, and he should be pleasuring her until she turned the tables and he called out her name.

Clenching her jaw, Lisa envisioned pulling in behind Keith's truck, ringing the doorbell, and then when Maddie opened the door, beating her until she could no longer stand. Once finished, she and Keith would have sex on the bitch's living room floor while she watched, unable to do anything about it. As satisfying as that might be, it would only accomplish one thing: a trip before a judge while wearing handcuffs. And the only handcuffs she wanted anyone placing on her wrists were the fuzzy black ones in her nightstand drawer.

"Stick to the plan."

She'd learned the importance of making a plan from her grandmother. It didn't matter if your end goal was to lose ten pounds, get the lead role in the school play, or save enough to buy a new house. According to her grandmother, as long as you created a plan, followed it, and modified it if and when necessary, you could achieve anything. And she'd taken the next step in it tonight when she'd asked the bitch if she had been at Murphy's earlier this week.

Since Maddie had never shown her a picture of Keith, it'd be impossible for Lisa to claim she'd seen him with another woman. But a solution to the problem fell into her lap Monday night. She'd stopped in Murphy's Tavern after driving by Keith's apartment complex and not seeing his car in the parking lot. Then, as if she'd conjured him up, he'd entered the tavern with another guy and walked right past her while she sat at the bar nursing a margarita. Fifteen minutes later, Maddie joined them.

With that minor obstacle out of the way, Lisa could claim she'd seen Keith with another woman and hopefully plant other seeds of doubt in Maddie's mind. Fingers crossed, she could do even more than that. As the old saying went, a picture was worth a thousand words. She even had the perfect woman in mind. Her cousin was always up for anything.

No matter if this current strategy worked, though, in the end, Lisa would get what she wanted, no matter how much she needed to change her plan.

THREE

At the sound of the doorbell, Maddie glanced at the spare key she'd taken out earlier and left on the counter. The same one she'd removed from the drawer last week and then put away rather than give it to Keith. Considering how often he came by, it made sense for him to have a key. But now, like last week, Maddie wondered if she should hold off on giving it to him.

Some people viewed the exchange of house keys as a significant step in a relationship. And maybe it was. Her brother was the only person she'd ever given her house key to, but Spencer had been living with her. If she gave it to Keith, he might add it to his key ring without a second thought. Or he might assume she expected more of a commitment from him. Since, as far as she knew, he'd never even referred to her as his girlfriend, such an assumption might be disastrous for their relationship.

Figure it out later.

It wasn't like the key could walk over and jump into Keith's hand. And if she put it back in the drawer tomorrow morning, so what? Next week, it would still be there if she decided the time was right.

After putting the cover on the pan, she lowered the heat and wiped her hands on a towel before leaving the kitchen. Only her closest friends and family knew it, but she loved cooking. It didn't matter if she was preparing chicken piccata for a sit-down meal with her family or whipping up some buffalo wings for a poker game with friends. Not only did the process relax her, but it also amazed her how she could take individual ingredients, sometimes ones that tasted disgusting alone, like raw onions, and combine them to make something delicious. Since work often made cooking anything fancier than pasta and store-bought meatballs impossible, she never passed up an opportunity when one popped up.

And Keith had dropped one in her lap Friday night. Or maybe his sister and her boyfriend deserved the credit. Whatever the case, Maddie had pointed out that dinner at her house might be more enjoyable for everyone. Brett Sherbrooke didn't draw the same amount of attention as some of his cousins, but his presence in a restaurant wouldn't go unnoticed, especially right now, since he was running for the United States Senate.

She'd started considering ideas for tonight's meal while Keith gave Jen her address. Then earlier today, when Keith left to meet Connor at the gym, she'd gone grocery shopping and then made a pit stop at Sugar and Spice Bakery before coming home. The desserts from there were the next best thing to homemade, and not once had anything she purchased disappointed her.

Maddie's eyes skipped past the bakery box Keith held and zeroed in on the flowers in his left hand when she opened the door.

Whatever the opposite of a green thumb was, she had it. No matter how hard Maddie tried, she killed every plant she brought home, regardless of whether she left it on a windowsill in the living room, in the kitchen, or in the backyard. But, despite her inability to keep anything in the plant kingdom alive, she liked flowers and house plants. Perhaps not as much as Alexandra, the only other female member of HRT, or Salty's girlfriend, but once or twice a month, she picked up an arrangement while grocery shopping to brighten up her house. Especially in the winter, when the days seemed dreary even when the sun was out.

Except for the get-well-soon bouquet her sister-in-law had sent after Maddie had been injured while on an assignment, she couldn't remember the last time someone gave her flowers. And Brittany had been the one behind the thoughtful gesture, not her brother, because Tucker never would've thought to send them.

"Did you miss me?" Keith's lips curved into a sexy grin, the very one that attracted women to him much the way a flame attracted a moth. Herself included.

"You left? I didn't even notice, but welcome back. It's nice to see you." Maddie pressed her lips together to keep from smiling as she patted his cheek.

"Only nice?" Keith asked, putting the flowers and the bakery box down on the table by the sofa. His hands now free, he settled one on her waist and cupped the back of her head with his other before claiming her lips. Slowly, his mouth moved over hers, each pass a little more intense than the one before it.

As if they had a mind of their own, her lips parted. When Keith's tongue touched hers, heat spiraled through her body, and she had a good idea of how the pan on the stove felt.

The buzzing timer ended any thoughts of continuing their reunion in her bedroom. Reluctantly, she pulled back, because if she didn't do it now, she wouldn't be able to, and then dinner would be ruined. Takeout was great, but not what she wanted to serve to Keith's sister and her boyfriend.

"Okay, it's really nice to see you." She patted his cheek a second time, then walked away before he distracted her again—something he excelled at even without touching her. Exactly how he managed it, she didn't know.

Keith entered the kitchen right after her, carrying the flowers and a large bakery box. "Whatever you're cooking, it smells amazing."

"Chicken marsala with pasta and homemade bread rolls."

She'd found the bread recipe on her favorite cooking website the only year she'd prepared Thanksgiving dinner for the family. Although a bit time-consuming because the dough needed to rise, it was a simple recipe and far better than any bread she found in the store. And before the rolls turned into hockey pucks, she pulled the baking pan out of the oven.

"I still need to make the Caprese salad. But that won't take long."

"Wow, you went all out tonight. You didn't have to. It's only my sister and Brett."

"Next time, I'll heat up some frozen pizzas and serve them with potato chips. Will that be better?"

"They'd be delicious compared to what Brett and I ate in the army."

She was aware of how Keith and Brett had become friends. Still, she sometimes had trouble reconciling that a billionaire from one of the most prominent families in America and who appeared in photos with individuals like Jake and Trent Sherbrooke had served in the military.

Keith waited until she pulled her oven mitts off before holding out the floral arrangement. "I wasn't sure what your favorite flowers were, so I asked the florist to put together something she'd like to get."

Although the only logical explanation for why he'd arrived with them was that he'd bought them for her, surprise kept Maddie from immediately accepting the flowers.

"You don't like them?" Disappointment laced his voice, and a subtle frown formed on his face.

A mixture of blue hydrangeas, cream roses, lilies, and a few other flowers she didn't recognize, the arrangement was far nicer than the ones she usually purchased while grocery shopping. "They're gorgeous. I just wasn't expecting flowers from you." They'd been honest with each other since the day they met; she saw no reason to stop now. "I never pictured you as a flower-giving type of person."

"Usually I'm not, unless you count the ones I send my mom on Mother's Day. Oh, and I guess I sent Bella some last year after she had her tonsils out."

She'd never met Bella, but she knew Keith adored his only niece.

"But you often buy yourself flowers, and you don't have any right now, so I thought you'd like some. If you don't want me to do it again, I won't."

"I love them. Later, when we have more time, I'll show you how much I appreciate them." She kissed his cheek, a much safer option than his lips because their guests should be there soon, and she still had work to do.

Keith's palms traveled down her arms before settling on her waist and tugging her closer. "I won't forget you said that." He whispered the words near her lips before kissing her. "After I left the florist, I went into the new bakery next door and got some desserts."

In her book, there was no such thing as too much dessert.

Less than fifteen minutes later, as she washed down the counter, the doorbell rang for a second time that night.

"I got it," Keith said before she could ask him to answer the door so she could finish cleaning.

A woman's voice reached her a few seconds later. "We would've been here about ten minutes ago, but there was an accident at the intersection of Maple and Grove. It looked like someone ran the red light."

Since she'd lived in the area, there seemed to be at least one accident at the intersection every month.

Maddie wouldn't have recognized the thirty-something-year-old woman who entered the kitchen six months ago. Unlike her, Keith didn't have family photos displayed in his apartment, and if his sister had visited him since he started working for Elite Force, she'd never met the woman. But, thanks to the media and the photos it had published ever since Jen and Brett began dating a few months ago, Maddie recognized Keith's youngest sister.

"Jen, Brett, I'd like you to meet my girlfriend, Maddie."

The counter behind her and years of trying to be prepared for anything kept her upright. Not even an hour ago, she'd been thinking about how Keith had never used the term, at least around her, and now he was introducing her to his sister as his girlfriend. Maybe their relationship could handle the exchange of house keys.

Some people were huggers, and others weren't. Jen fell into the first category. "I've heard a lot about you. It's great to meet you and finally put a face to the name. Thank you for having us over tonight," she said, embracing Maddie.

The other woman's greeting raised all kinds of questions. Maddie couldn't put her finger on exactly why, but Jen's tone when she said "finally meet you" gave Maddie the impression Keith had mentioned her before they started dating. And what did "a lot" entail? Had he talked about the team as a whole and shared info about everyone? Or had he singled her out? And if so, what had he told his sister?

Although Spencer had met Keith, she'd never talked to her brother about him. And she didn't think Tucker even knew Keith existed. The only person she'd shared specific details about him with was her younger sister, Autumn—something Maddie often wished she'd never done. Right up until Autumn learned they'd kissed in Maddie's kitchen, every chance Autumn got, she'd encouraged her to pursue him despite the fact they worked together.

Despite being more of the handshaking type, Maddie returned Jen's hug. After all, what other choice did she have? "Anytime. You could say cooking is a hobby of mine, but I don't get to do it as often as I'd like."

"I'm sure my brother loves that. Keith's out of luck if it requires much more than boiling water or popping something in the microwave."

"How many times have I grilled steaks and burgers at your house?" Keith asked.

"Cooking and grilling are not the same things."

The topic didn't require Maddie's input, but she gave it anyway. "Your sister is technically right, Keith."

"Don't bother, Keith; you're not going to win this one," Brett said when it appeared Keith planned to press the matter. "We didn't know what you were preparing."

Brett handed her a bottle of chardonnay and a cabernet. She didn't recognize the names on the labels, but she'd bet her monthly salary they both cost three times more than what she bought.

"The chardonnay is perfect. Thank you." She had white and red wine on hand if they needed more than one bottle. "Dinner is ready. If the three of you want to sit down, I'll bring everything in."

Since the room was small and she lived alone, she'd opted for a small pub-style table that only accommodated two in the kitchen rather than a full-size table and chairs set. She used the dining room if and when she had more than one guest. Although not an enormous room either, she'd found a dining room nook set that fit well in the corner and seated six if she added the extra table leaf.

"I'll give you a hand," Jen said.

She didn't need the help, but she wasn't going to look a gift horse in the mouth either, as her mom would say. If Jen stayed, it would give Maddie a chance to ask a few of the questions from her list—a rather long list that included not only Keith but Jen and Brett's relationship.

Keith had told her Jen and Brett's initial friendship had started via a letter his sister had included in her girl scout troop's care packages to Keith and Brett's unit. A closet romantic, with the romance novels to prove it, Maddie wanted to know more. What had it been like when they finally met face-to-face? Who'd made the first move out of the friend zone?

Rather than get her butt into gear, Maddie considered what to ask first and admired Keith's ass as he and Brett walked away. It truly was something to marvel at.

"What can I do?" Jen asked, interrupting Maddie's visual inspection.

"Can you get me the large glass bowl from the cabinet next to the fridge... and maybe answer a few questions?" Maddie answered as she transferred the chicken to a serving dish.

"You got it, as long as I get to ask one or two of my own."

Fair was fair. And it wasn't like she had anything to hide. "Deal."

"What do you want to know?" Jen asked.

It was more like what didn't she want to know, but they only had so much time. "I know about the care packages and the letters, but what was it like when you finally saw Brett face-to-face?"

"I expected questions about Keith, but okay. I'd say it was nerve-racking. Actually, I almost canceled on him several times," she answered, putting the bowl down next to the stove. "And the afternoon we met, I even thought about leaving the cafe before he arrived."

"What stopped you?"

Even as a kid, meeting new people had never fazed her—a definite plus in her line of work. But maybe if she'd been in Jen's situation, it would've made her a little uneasy.

"I kept reminding myself that after almost two years of exchanging letters and text messages, I practically knew him already. And that worse case, we had coffee together and then never saw each other again."

"Two years. Wow, I didn't realize you'd been writing back and forth to each other for so long."

"Keith didn't either. I didn't tell him until after Brett asked me to spend the day with him."

That bit of information, he hadn't shared with her. "You didn't leave, so what happened once he got there?"

"Almost as soon as he sat down, it was like I was having

coffee with any other friend." Jen leaned against the counter and shrugged. "Well, more or less. Brett tends to get noticed by people, especially women. And there were plenty checking him out that night."

She could see why. Maddie wasn't single, but she had perfect eyesight, and Brett Sherbrooke was gorgeous. Based on the little Keith had shared about his friend, Brett was more than a handsome face with boatloads of cash. He was a nice guy too.

"I feel your pain. I've noticed women doing the same to Keith."

"Yeah, but then my brother opens his big mouth, and they all decide he's not worth it."

Maddie added the last of the chicken to the dish. "Nah, I think it's his ego that's the problem."

Jen nodded as her smile grew wider. "Good point. Sometimes I don't know how his head fits through doorways. But Keith can be sweet and thoughtful when he wants to be. Loyal too."

"It sounds like he has a lot in common with a dog."

"Now that you mention it, he does. But Keith has slightly better table manners. Hopefully, better breath too."

With the chicken ready to be carried in, she turned her attention to the pasta. "Okay, so I got in two questions. Now, it's your turn," Maddie said, carrying the pot to the sink so she could drain the water.

The rest of her list would have to wait. If they stayed in the kitchen much longer, Keith would wonder what was taking so long and come investigate. The guy could be nosey like that.

"Did you make the first move, or did my brother finally put his big-boy pants on?"

An image of Keith dressed like a young schoolboy in the early twentieth century popped up, and Maddie burst out laughing. "No, he put on his big-boy pants," she answered once she could speak again.

"Took him long enough."

Rather than removing them, their conversation added more questions to her list. "Later, you and I need to talk more." Maddie gestured toward the chicken. "If you can bring that and the rolls in, I can handle everything else."

"Sure thing, but before we go into the other room…." Jen paused and peeked around the doorway. "Well, you've known Keith for a while, so you probably already know this, but my brother has always been more of a casual dater. I only remember him having three girlfriends. One was in high school. Melinda went to school with us. Kristen was even on the swim team with her, so she doesn't count. And he had two in college."

It surprised Maddie he'd even had that many.

"And you're the first girlfriend he's ever wanted any of us to meet."

KEITH GLANCED TOWARD THE HALLWAY. It was taking them a hell of a lot longer than necessary to get food transferred from the stove to a dish. Knowing Maddie, she'd asked Jen to share all his most embarrassing moments, and his sister was sharing all the ones she remembered.

"It's about time," Keith muttered when he saw the two women exit the kitchen.

"Is that desperation I hear in your voice?" Brett asked. "Afraid your sister is spilling all your secrets?"

"Just hungry."

"Hey, it could be worse. At least it's just Jen in there with Maddie. Your sister has met almost my entire family, including my cousins Jake and Trent. And you know what they're like."

He'd seen both men at Brett's place when the guy still lived in Virginia. They'd gone above and beyond the call of duty when it came to busting their cousin's balls. And Brett had given it right back to them. It'd made him wish for a brother or some close male cousins.

"I don't think there are any embarrassing stories about me left that Jen hasn't heard," Brett said.

Keith watched Maddie and Jen walk toward the dining room. "I might have to ask my sister to share some."

"You can ask, but I don't see Jen doing it."

His sister placed the rolls and chicken on the table and then pulled out a chair. "What don't you see me doing?"

"Retelling those delightful stories about me that my family shared with you."

"Don't worry. Your secrets are safe with me." Jen patted Brett's hand before smiling at her brother. "Sorry, Keith, you're my brother, and I love you, but—"

"She loves me more." Putting his arm around her shoulders, Brett kissed her cheek.

Brett made the list of his friends Keith would ever want his sister to date. Admittedly, it was an incredibly short list. But despite the recent photos and his brief visit to New England, Keith still found it odd to see his longtime friend kissing his baby sister.

Across the table, Jen shook her head and accepted the salad Maddie held toward her. "My brother isn't the only one with a big ego."

It was time to move the conversation along before either woman started listing his many faults. "Are you two sticking around for a few days?"

"We're heading back tomorrow. I have a town hall forum at noon on Tuesday and a meet and greet with a veterans' group later that night," Brett replied.

Keith would rather live in a cave, eating nothing but insects for the rest of his life, than enter the snake pit on Capitol Hill. Honestly, he didn't understand why anyone, including Brett, would. But that didn't mean he wasn't interested in how his buddy's bid for the late Senator Brown's seat was going.

"How's the campaign going?"

"The polls now have me with a ten-point lead over Smith.

When the truth came out, I think his stunt killed whatever chance he had with most voters."

He'd wanted to kill the sleazy bastard when Ted Smith's campaign leaked the bullshit story about Jen to the media.

"With that kind of lead, it sounds like you've got your party's nomination in the bag," Maddie said.

They'd never discussed politics specifically, but Keith knew her views aligned with his based on comments she'd made regarding issues and various people in DC.

"Until the votes are in, nothing is definite, but it looks that way. My campaign team has already started shifting gears and is working on my strategy for the election in December. That was one of the reasons I met with my uncle today."

When your uncle was President Warren Sherbrooke, a former United States Senator and so well-liked that every political analyst assumed he would easily win a second term, you'd be stupid not to ask him for advice. And Brett was a lot of things, but stupid wasn't one of them.

"Do you think you'll be facing Hammond or Reed in December?" Keith asked as he reached for another roll. The things were too damn good to stop at one.

Although it was taking place in Massachusetts, the special election was getting national attention, so unless you lived under a rock, you knew who the two candidates hoping to get the other party's nomination were. Gina Hammond was a career politician who'd lost her Senate bid in Vermont last year, then moved to Massachusetts to try again, while Vince Reed was a former professional football player turned successful businessman.

"They're virtually tied in the polls," Brett replied. "But I think Hammond is going to win the nomination."

Brett's campaign and the upcoming election dominated the conversation for several more minutes before Jen not so subtly changed the subject. Considering that his sister probably ate, slept, and breathed politics these days, he couldn't fault her for wanting to talk about something else.

"So, Maddie, has my brother been behaving himself?" she asked. "If he hasn't been, our mom offered to come down and set him straight for you."

Mom would do it too. When it came to her children, Erica Wallace didn't care how old they were. If Mom thought you'd fucked up, she told you so. And Keith would know; he'd been on the receiving end of her displeasure more than once. The same was true of his father, except Reggie Wallace used less polite language to get across the same message.

"I can try too, but it probably won't do much good. Keith doesn't usually listen to me," Jen said.

"Must be an older-brother thing. I've got two, and they're the same way."

"No, in Keith's case, I think the words I use are too complicated for him to understand." Jen winked at him as she spoke. "I often forget Keith's vocabulary is similar to that of a ten-year-old. That's probably why he gets along so well with our niece, Bella."

"Ten, huh? I would've put it closer to twelve. But you've known Keith a lot longer, so I'll defer to you. His limited vocabulary aside, though, he's been a good boy. He even brought me these tonight." Maddie pointed her fork at the flowers he'd picked up earlier.

"Nicely done, Keith. They're gorgeous. I'll let Mom know she can hold off on driving here and giving you a lecture."

FOUR

Keith watched the fire he'd started lick at the dry wood. There were definite perks to living where he did. He didn't need to worry about yard maintenance or shoveling out his car if it snowed. When large ticket items like the central AC or the heat died, it was someone else's responsibility to repair it. One downside, though, he couldn't crack a cold one and relax outside with a fire like he was doing now. At his place, the best he could do was sit on the small balcony off his living room and watch the cars coming and going from the parking lot below.

Satisfied the fire was good for the moment, he grabbed the beer he'd left on the table as his sister placed a tray containing cups, a carafe of coffee, and a plate of desserts on it.

"Hey, where are the chocolate éclairs? I bought two." They were his favorite pastry, and neither were on the plate. His sister loved them too, and he wouldn't put it past her to eat them before anyone else got a chance.

With his preferred dessert not present, he eyed the assortment, which consisted of various types of cannoli, lemon squares, and the seven-layer magic bars he'd picked up. When it came to cannoli, he was picky. If made the traditional way with ricotta cheese, he never touched the things. But earlier, he'd noticed the box from Sugar and Spice, so these were from there. While the bakery sold ones filled with cheese, it used cream for its chocolate ones. And if Keith had a weakness for any single food, it was chocolate, no matter the kind or how it was served.

"If you ate them, you need to go get me more right now," Keith said, selecting a mini chocolate cannoli for now.

"Relax. Everything didn't fit on one plate. Maddie's going to bring out the rest. She got a phone call from her mom."

"They better be."

"I'm going to pretend you didn't say that." Jen glanced back at the door as she added cream and sugar to her coffee. "You were right. I like Maddie a lot."

Although Jen had insisted she didn't need him to come home when the bullshit story about her being arrested as a kid came out, he'd taken a few days off and gone to see her anyway. It hadn't mattered to him that she had the support of Brett and the Sherbrooke family, as well as their parents. She was his kid sister, and he needed to make sure she was okay. During a late-night talk that involved pints of chocolate ice cream topped with crushed-up double chocolate chip cookies, he'd first used the words "Maddie" and "girlfriend" in the same sentence. Girlfriend wasn't normally a word in his vocabulary, so he'd expected Jen to be surprised or maybe even accuse him of joking around. Instead, his sister told him it was about time they got together and then explained how she'd known for months that he had it bad for Maddie.

"Mom and Dad are going to love her. Kristen too. Is she coming to Thanksgiving with you?"

Keith hadn't thought much about the upcoming holiday, and Maddie hadn't mentioned it. Unfortunately, he'd probably missed more Thanksgivings in the past twelve years than he'd made it to. A perk of leaving active duty and taking the position with Elite Force was the ability to see his family, maybe not for every holiday, but at least most. Assuming an assignment didn't prevent him from traveling to New England, he'd like to celebrate Thanksgiving with his family and Maddie. She might want to spend it with hers, though.

"We haven't talked about it, so I don't know what we're doing for Thanksgiving yet. But next week we're going to Maine for the weekend. So we're going to stop and see Mom and Dad then." With Jen's question answered, he bit into the chocolate-cream-filled pastry.

About to take a sip of coffee, his sister paused at his announcement. "Considering it must be at least an eight-hour drive to Maine from here, it's an odd choice for a weekend getaway."

"Colby is getting married, and the other night, he asked me to be his best man," Keith explained as he licked chocolate cream off his thumb. "We're flying into Providence Friday night and then driving up to Ogunquit."

"Typical Colby, waiting until the last minute to ask you."

The guy had been a permanent fixture at their house in high school, so Jen and Kristen had gotten to know him well. And Colby was the king of doing things at the last moment.

"Sorry about that. Mom was chatty tonight." Maddie handed him an éclair before putting the rest of the desserts on the table. "Why didn't you ever tell me you were in a band, Keith?"

Considering the intel Jen could've divulged about him, the fact he'd played in a band while in high school and college wasn't the worst.

"Just didn't think of it." His days performing seemed like a lifetime ago, and he rarely thought about them.

"I've got some videos of you performing, including when you played at the talent show your senior year. And when I get home, I'm going to dig them out and send them to Maddie."

He'd rather have his sister share videos of him with his old band than ones Mom probably had of him as a baby walking around in a diaper.

"Not before I get a chance to watch them." Brett selected the other éclair before Keith could get his hands on it and held it up as if to toast him before splitting it and handing half to Jen.

Damn it.

He should've ordered only éclairs instead of getting an assortment of desserts. "Share whatever you want. Just remember, I can do the same. And I remember some pretty bad high school yearbook pictures."

"When was the last time you saw your picture from freshman year?" Jen asked.

Thanks to the varsity football players, it had been his worst school photo ever. And that was saying something.

"Can't be any worse than mine," Maddie replied. "I don't think there is a person alive with a good freshman yearbook picture."

"You'd be surprised. The varsity athletes, well the boys, used to do what they called freshman cuts on the morning of school pictures. Keith has random sections of his hair shaved off in his picture. Mom was furious when she saw him."

"High school boys aren't known for their intelligence." Maddie nudged him with her elbow. "Did you do it to freshmen when you were an upperclassman?"

Even back then, he'd thought it a stupid thing to do. "No, the administration cracked down on it the following year and suspended anyone caught doing it."

His teammates had been pissed about it. But while he'd complained along with them, he'd been happy to see the dumb tradition end.

PULLING THE SHEET UP, Maddie tucked it around herself. Although she had no qualms about being naked, she was suddenly chilly and too comfortable to get up and put on clothes. "Are you staying here tonight?"

Often when Keith came over, he ended up spending the

night. But while she knew what her schedule looked like in the morning, she didn't know about his. Depending on what he needed to do, he might not have the time to stop at home and get ready before heading to work, and other than some toiletries, he didn't have anything here, which was something else she wanted to talk to him about. She'd never been big into clothes, so she had plenty of closet and drawer space for him to leave some extra clothes here. She'd held off bringing it up because, like with the house key, she worried it might send Keith running for the closest exit.

"Do you want me to?"

Talk about a stupid question.

"I wouldn't have asked if I didn't."

Rolling onto his side, Keith draped an arm across her stomach. "Looks like you have a roommate for the night. Next time I get up, I'll go out and grab my bag from my truck."

"Why didn't you bring it in when you got back?"

"I wasn't sure you'd want me to stay, and you know what they say about assuming things," he answered as his fingertips brushed up and down her arm.

Some openings were too good to resist, and that was definitely one. "You make an ass of yourself all the time; why should tonight be any different?"

Keith's fingers stopped as he propped himself up on an elbow and frowned at her. "Sounds like something Jen would say. I'm not surprised you two got along so well tonight."

"Or you'd say. Admit it. You wouldn't have passed up the opportunity if I'd said the same thing."

"I plead the fifth."

"Whatever. Seriously though, I love when you spend the night." It was the first time she'd ever put the L-word and him in the same sentence. "I think you should leave some clothes here so you can do it whenever you want."

"Sometime this week, I'll bring stuff over. Next time you come to my place, you should do the same thing."

What the hell? Just do it.

"Since you're here so much, you might as well have a key. I left one on the counter in the kitchen. Don't let me forget to give it to you in the morning."

Keith didn't bolt out of bed. "Will do. We spend more time here, but I'll find the spare key to my apartment for you."

"It's probably in that junk drawer of yours." She'd stumbled upon it while looking for utensils one night. It contained everything from batteries and disposable chopsticks from the local Chinese restaurant to computer cables.

"Hey, don't knock on my junk drawer. You're the only person I know who doesn't have at least one. Hell, Jen has three."

He had a point. Most people did have at least one, her parents included.

"Somehow, I don't see Brett having one." She'd only spent a few hours with the guy, but she got the impression he didn't like clutter.

"Yeah, if another person in the world exists besides you that doesn't have one, it'd be him." Keith shook his head ever so slightly as his fingers moved up and down her arm again. "I'm still getting used to him and my sister being together."

Maybe it was the romantic in her, but after seeing the couple together and talking to Jen, she didn't see them splitting up. "You're going to have plenty of time to get comfortable with it. I see wedding bells in their future."

"Brett's a great guy, and I'd trust him with my life, but I wouldn't want to marry into that family. The fucking media never leaves them alone. They can't even get a damn haircut without the internet talking about it."

Although an exaggeration, it wasn't too far from the truth. "Jen told me about a few run-ins she's had with the media. And before you ask, no, there's nothing you need to worry about."

"Considering how much time you two spent alone, I'm sure it's not the only thing she shared."

"Don't worry. Your sister didn't tell me all the stupid things you did as a kid."

"Yeah, I doubt that."

"Actually, Jen and I talked more about her and Brett. How they met is like a story from a romance novel. They'd been writing to each other for months before your sister even realized Brett was President Sherbrooke's nephew."

"Like a story from a romance novel? I think there's something you're not telling me." The corners of his lips inched ever so slightly upward. And Maddie expected a teasing grin at any moment.

"You watch the Hallmark Channel and read books by Nora Roberts when you're alone, don't you?" Keith gently pinched her arm and grinned.

She'd opened her big mouth. "When it comes to the Hallmark Channel, I plead the fifth. As far as Nora Roberts goes, I've read none of her books." Nana, whom she often shared romance novels with, loved Nora Roberts' work, but none of the author's storylines appealed to Maddie. "How do you even know who Nora Roberts is?"

"My mom's a romance junkie. She could start a bookstore with all the paperbacks she has."

Maddie tucked the tidbit of information away. Then, if she found herself alone with Keith's mom when they visited and couldn't think of anything else, she'd put it to use.

FIVE

DAMN IT. HE'S STILL THERE.

Lisa punched the car door as she drove past Maddie's house again. The first time, she'd turned onto the bitch's street in time to see a black sedan park behind Keith's truck. Rather than continue, Lisa had pulled over and pretended to talk on her phone. But, unfortunately, she hadn't gotten a good enough look at the driver's face as he walked around to the passenger side to know if it was one of the guys Keith often met at Murphy's Tavern. Whoever the couple was, Keith knew the woman, because he'd hugged her when he opened the front door.

The couple's identity didn't matter, anyway. The fact Keith's truck remained, and it appeared as if all the lights inside Maddie's house were off, did.

An image of Keith sucking on Maddie's nipples while he slipped his finger in and out of her like he used to do to her formed, and Lisa screeched as she sped down the street. He shouldn't be in there with the bitch.

She slammed on the brakes and closed her eyes when she reached the stop sign. Taking a deep breath, she forced out the image of Keith and Maddie and replaced it with a different one. One where Keith handcuffed her to her bed and then used his tongue to make her come. Need ripped through her body. While she could walk into Shooter's or Murphy's and leave with someone who'd satisfy her body, she didn't want some random guy. She wanted Keith. If she couldn't have him, Lisa would take care of her own needs when she got home. She had more than enough toys to make it happen.

No, she'd do more than that.

Smiling, Lisa turned left. The next message Keith received would include more than words. A short video of her pleasuring herself would accompany it. Lisa didn't know if Maddie had read the past messages. But fingers crossed, she'd see this, because no girlfriend wanted their guy receiving sex videos from another woman. Even if the bitch didn't see it, the video would remind Keith of what he was missing by not being with her.

Three hours later, Lisa sat at the kitchen table, her body satisfied, reviewing the videos she'd taken as her cousin came home.

"Faster." Lisa's voice, followed by a moan, filled the room, and Nicole stopped next to the table.

"That sounded like you. What are you watching, Lis?"

"A little something for Keith to remind him of what he's missing." Finishing her wine, Lisa refilled her glass. "Do you want some?"

"Sure, why not," Nicole said, grabbing a glass and a box of rosemary crackers off the counter. "What have you been up to all night? Well, besides that." Nicole gestured toward the iPad as she accepted the wine bottle and filled her glass.

Her cousin knew Lisa wanted Keith back. Nicole also knew about the text messages and that she regularly staked out the places he frequented, hoping to see him. But Nicole didn't know Lisa had not only learned the identity of Keith's new girlfriend and where she lived but had also befriended her.

"Not much."

Thanks to her cheating ex-husband, Nicole now considered one guy just as good as the next. She didn't understand the connection between Keith and Lisa. Nicole insisted Lisa was mistaking lust for love. According to her cousin, the quickest way for her to get over Keith was to get screwed until she couldn't walk straight by the hottest guy she could find. So if Lisa told Nicole she'd spent time finding out where Keith was, her cousin would give her another lecture about how she'd wasted another night.

"You should've come with me," Nicole said before taking a sip of wine.

"Was the band any good?"

Every weekend, The Raven, a downtown club, featured live music. While she'd enjoyed most of the bands she'd heard perform, once in a while a group performed that shouldn't be playing anywhere other than in a soundproofed garage.

"Yeah. We've seen that band play there before," Nicole answered as she opened the cracker box. "And Shawn stopped in with a few of his friends. I don't know where he meets them, but your stepbrother has the hottest friends."

Nicole wasn't wrong. She'd yet to meet a friend of her stepbrother's that was ugly.

"Any of them would have you saying, 'Keith who?' But especially Jeremy, I think. He's built a little like Keith, and he's got the most incredible eyes. They're this crazy ice-blue. I've never seen anything like them."

Over the years, she'd hooked up with more than one of Shawn's friends. Her cousin had as well. But she hadn't spent time with any of them, or any guy for that matter, since Keith.

"I've met Jeremy." The guy's unique eye color alone made him impossible to forget. "He reminds me of the model who does the watch commercial. You know, the one where he dives into a rooftop pool and then kicks to the surface. I don't remember what brand it is."

Of course, she didn't remember Jeremy only because of his eyes. Three years ago, he'd helped Lisa make the obstacle standing between her and the small reoccurring role on *Precinct 3*, a cop drama that unfortunately only lasted one season, disappear. And if she needed to make the same thing happen with Maddie, she'd be enlisting his aid again.

"Yeah, you're right. Jeremy does resemble that model."

"Did you go home with him after the show?" Before meeting Keith, if Jeremy had invited her over, Lisa wouldn't have turned him down.

Shaking her head, Nicole took several crackers from the box and then pushed it closer to Lisa. "Shawn and I went back to his place."

For the past two years, her cousin and Shawn had an on-again-off-again arrangement. So whenever Shawn was single, which frequently happened because the guy got bored fast and wanted sex, he turned to Nicole. Her cousin happily obliged every time—not that Lisa entirely blamed her. An amateur MMA fighter, her stepbrother had a face that belonged on the billboards in Times Square and the body to match. And according to Nicole, he was the best lover she'd ever had, which was why she never said no when he came knocking.

"I'm guessing that means he'll be over this week?"

She'd lived with her cousin long enough to know the routine. Nicole preferred the townhouse to herself when Shawn came over, and if she knew in advance, Lisa found things to do away from home. Nicole reciprocated when Lisa brought a guy home, which was why she'd never met Keith. The one time she had seen Keith, she'd been pulling into the garage as Keith walked out the front door.

"Probably, but I'm not sure when. He's working on a project."

Interesting way to phrase it.

Shawn had never shared the exact details. However, he'd told her enough, so Lisa knew his work involved providing the information he got by hacking companies and organizations to whoever had hired him. Based on his lifestyle, those people paid well.

"If you give me a heads-up, I'll find somewhere to go," Lisa said.

"I'll try. You know how last-minute Shawn can be." Nicole raised her wineglass. Before the glass reached her mouth, she put it back down. "You probably don't want to hear this, but I truly think it's time to forget about Keith."

Yep, she didn't want to hear it tonight. They'd already had this conversation, and nothing Nicole said now would change her mind.

"It's been months since you saw him."

Well, it had been months since they'd been together, but she got her cousin's point.

"You need to start looking for someone else instead of wasting your time waiting for something that might never happen."

Oh, it'll happen.

Lisa adored her cousin, but the woman just didn't understand. A connection like the one between her and Keith was rare. But Nicole was right about wasting time, though, because every damn day that went by and they weren't together was a waste. Hopefully, when Keith opened her little present, Maddie would be there. It might not end their relationship immediately, but it would raise some red flags in Maddie's head while at the same time reminding Keith of what he was missing out on every night. And if it didn't, there was something seriously wrong with the woman. If Keith had received a similar video when they were together, she would've taught him a lesson he wouldn't soon forget.

"Trust me. We'll get back together."

Nicole gave her an if-you-say-so look but didn't argue. "Do you think he's still with the woman you saw him with at Murphy's?"

Biting into a cracker, Lisa scowled. "Yeah. I saw them there again last night." But, of course, she couldn't tell Nicole where she'd really seen them without telling her she knew where Maddie lived.

"Too bad it's illegal to make sure someone has a little 'accident,'" Nicole said, using air quotes.

Illegal or not, she'd done it before, and she wasn't opposed to doing it again soon. But, again, some things she couldn't share with Nicole. "Tell me about it. But with some luck, Keith's girlfriend will see this video when I send it to him."

"I'd be pissed off if I found something like that on my guy's phone. But he might delete it before she finds it."

"He'll keep it so he can watch it whenever he wants."

"You're probably right. When it comes to porn, guys are pigs."

She still hadn't determined how to make it happen, but a picture of Keith with another woman would go a long way to driving him and Maddie apart.

"I don't know how to get it, but I want a picture of Keith with another woman that I can send to his girlfriend. If I can figure out a way to set him up, will you help me?"

"Happy to help." Nicole narrowed her eyes as she rested her arms on the table. "But how do you plan to get the picture to the girlfriend?"

Idiot. She'd spoken without thinking.

"Maddie goes to my gym." Lisa shrugged as she decided how much to share. "We've gotten kind of friendly, and I have her phone number."

"Huh, well, if you figure out a way to get him and me at the same place, you can take all the pictures you need."

SIX

Everyone should live by the motto "Don't do stupid things, don't go to stupid places, and don't hang around with stupid people." But, unfortunately, far too many people didn't. Most of the time, it wasn't the end of the world. Occasionally, though, people found themselves in dangerous and sometimes deadly situations because they did one or all three of those things.

That had indeed been the case for Isla Doyle, the daughter of Elijah Doyle. An entrepreneur involved in everything from electric cars to technology for the military, no matter what the guy touched, it turned into money. And he had the private jet, expensive cars, and estates around the world to prove it.

Keith didn't blame the twenty-one-year-old college student for going barhopping with her friends. He'd done it in college, and he'd bet his savings account most people had at least once. But he'd never allowed himself to get so drunk he couldn't stand on his own. More importantly, he'd never left a bar with people he didn't know.

According to the surveillance videos Elite Force got from the bar and neighboring establishments, Isla had done both things on Saturday night. And although she'd arrived with friends that night, none had tried to stop her from leaving. With friends like that, who needed enemies?

Even worse, her roommate hadn't bothered to report her missing when Sunday night rolled around and Isla still hadn't returned to the apartment they shared, so no one even knew the young woman was in trouble.

Instead, Elijah Doyle received a phone call from the kidnappers Monday morning informing him they had his daughter and what they wanted from him. Anyone else would have immediately called the local police. Not Doyle. He'd called Eric Coleman, Elite Force Security's director and a longtime friend.

Within an hour of the call, Keith, along with five other members of HRT and two who he considered magicians from the cyber division, boarded one of Elite Force's company jets and headed for Miami. Honestly, the men and women who worked in the cyber division amazed him with the information they could get their hands on and how quickly they could do it.

Late Monday night, thanks in no small part to the cyber division's intel, the team located Isla holed up in a house with the two men the surveillance cameras had captured her leaving the bar with, as well as a third man—a campus police officer who, it turned out, had been following Isla's movements since the start of the fall semester.

This morning before sunrise, Keith led the team, backed up by local LEOs, into the house. They wouldn't involve outside agencies if it were up to him, but Coleman insisted on bringing them in. According to him, if Elite Force involved them, it allowed the firm to stay on their good side and, more importantly, know what they were up to. Nothing could fuck up a rescue mission worse than a local cop walking into a place he or she didn't belong.

Thankfully, the rescue went as planned, and the only people who suffered any injuries were the three kidnappers. He wasn't a medical expert, but what those two guys from the surveillance video received hadn't looked life-threatening. Unfortunately, he couldn't say the same about the third guy. Judging by the amount of blood he'd lost, it didn't look good for him. More importantly, though, while Isla had been upset—who wouldn't be?—she had not been physically harmed. Unfortunately, all too often, that wasn't the case.

The team packed up and headed home as soon as the police took possession of the crime scene, and Keith escorted Isla to her father and a medical team who'd been waiting at a nearby safe location.

Two hours after landing, they remained in the team conference room, giving Ax a post-mission report.

"Does anyone have anything to add?" Ax asked from his usual spot at the conference table.

As mission leader, Keith had already given Ax a verbal report, and tomorrow, he'd do up an official written version. But Ax never relied on one person's recounting of events. Not because he didn't trust every member of the team, but because he knew firsthand that no one person saw everything during a mission. Throw some adrenaline into the mix, and you never know how complete a person's memory might be of an event.

The phone on the table rang before anyone responded. For all the technology Elite Force possessed, it still used old-fashioned office phones inside the building.

Ax's expression never changed as he listened to the caller. "You too," Ax said before hanging up the phone and clasping his hands together. "Coleman got an update from Miami PD. Gallagher made it through surgery and is in the ICU."

It always amazed Keith what doctors could do. He hadn't expected Ty Gallagher, the campus police officer, to even survive the trip to the hospital, never mind make it through surgery.

Not one to waste time, Ax went back to where they'd been before the interruption. "Unless one of you has something to add, we're done here." Then, when no one spoke up, he pushed back his chair. "See you all tomorrow."

"I have never seen Ax leave that fast," Matt said after their boss left the room.

The guy usually stuck around and bullshitted with them after debriefs and meetings. And although technically HRT's boss, it wasn't uncommon for him to attend any cookouts and poker games the team members hosted.

"Date?" Alexandra, or Alex as everyone called her, asked.

"If he has one, it's about time," Connor replied, coming to his feet.

Keith agreed. Nine months ago, Ax's long-term girlfriend called it quits when she relocated to Seattle, and Ax refused to go with her. As far as any of them knew, the guy hadn't gone out with anyone since then.

A knowing grin spread across Spike's face. "Looks like Ax isn't the only one in a rush tonight. Becca must be home."

"She got back this morning," Connor answered.

Keith wouldn't be sitting around here either if Maddie was home instead of in New York again with the countess and her granddaughter. Over the weekend, the two women had accepted an invitation to an art exhibit by a world-famous artist. Exactly why the chick was so famous, Keith had no idea because, to him, the paintings resembled something done by a three-year-old. Yet people paid millions of dollars for the woman's work. So Monday afternoon, they'd flown to New York City. While there, Violet insisted they see a Broadway show that had opened the previous week before returning to DC the next day.

"Surprised you're not already in the parking lot, Salty. Is Kenzie working late tonight?" Matt asked.

Nodding, Salty stood but didn't walk toward the door. "Yeah, she swapped shifts with someone who needed the night off. But by the time I pick up some takeout, she should be home."

Although something he did a lot, Keith didn't feel like grabbing takeout and eating it alone in his apartment. "Does anyone want to head to Murphy's?"

Alex nodded as she stood. "I could go for some of their Irish chips. But I want to stop home and change first."

They all wore the team's unofficial uniform of black tactical pants and dark T-shirts. Even when he wasn't working, Keith wore similar clothes, but not Alex. The woman loved color; she even drove a pink car. So it didn't surprise him Alex wanted to change before going anywhere.

"Why not? I've got nothing else to do. But I need to stop home before I head over too," Spike replied.

Spike lived alone and didn't have any pets, so Keith wondered why he needed to go home first, but whatever. The guy didn't have to answer to him.

"Matt?"

"Not tonight."

Since he had no reason to go anywhere else first, Keith stopped at his desk long enough to type up a preliminary mission report and then headed straight for Murphy's Tavern.

The summer between his junior and senior years at URI, he'd spent three weeks touring Ireland and Scotland with his mother because, not only couldn't Dad take that much time off from work, he hadn't wanted his wife to go alone. During the trip, they visited countless historical sights and museums but also local pubs. Every time he walked into Murphy's Tavern, it reminded him of that trip and the various establishments they'd eaten at.

Hardwood floors that appeared as though they'd seen countless footsteps covered the floor, and dark wood paneling covered most of the interior walls. An enormous bar occupied one section of the restaurant. According to the plaque mounted on it, the restaurant owners had rescued the bar from a much older establishment in Dublin, Ireland, before the building's new owners demolished and moved it here. While the bar added to the atmosphere, Keith doubted it'd been worth the cost. Tables and booths of varying sizes provided more indoor seating. A small stage area occupied the one brick wall in the joint, and every Thursday was karaoke night, while the tavern brought in musicians on Saturday nights. Sometimes they played traditional Irish music, but not always. Various family crests, photos of Irish rugby and soccer teams, and signs in Gaelic decorated the walls, making customers feel as though they'd entered a pub on the other side of the Atlantic.

Despite being a Tuesday night, the place was busy. Customers occupied even the tables on the patio, a section the owners had added back in the spring despite the cooler temperature. There wasn't an empty stool at the bar, either. With his preferred booth unavailable, which gave him a bird's-eye view of the entrance, Keith opted for a booth near the empty stage. Within moments of sitting down, an employee approached the table.

Keith accepted the menu Junior—according to his name tag—handed him. "I'm expecting two friends."

"I'll come back with extra place settings and two more menus. Can I bring you something to drink while you wait for them?"

Alex and Spike wouldn't wait for him to get his ass there before ordering, and neither would expect him to wait for them.

"Yeah, I'll have whatever IPA you have on tap." Yeah, he was sitting in an Irish restaurant, so he should probably order a Guinness, but he much preferred IPAs. "And also, an order of Irish chips."

Wedge fries smothered with Irish bacon, cheese curds, and a Montreal-style poutine gravy, the Irish chips were his favorite appetizer on the menu. Alex had also mentioned them back at headquarters. If he ordered some now, she might be here when they arrived. The order was certainly big enough for the three of them to share.

"I'll be right back with your drink," Junior said before leaving.

Keith noticed the tall blonde with boobs that didn't quit walking in his general direction out of the corner of his eye as he opened his menu. Wearing a short denim skirt and a tight top with a plunging neckline, the woman screamed "look at me." A glance at the nearby tables verified that several customers were doing precisely that. Too bad Matt wasn't there. The blonde was the type he usually went after.

Do I want the bangers and mash or the— The warm body suddenly pressed against him and the subtle flowery scent brought Keith's thoughts to a screeching halt.

"You looked lonely over here, so I thought I'd come over and see if you'd like some company tonight." The blonde's long, slender fingers, complete with bloodred fingertips, closed around his wrist. "I'm by myself too, and my roommate isn't home tonight."

Before he could process her intention, the blonde moved his hand off the table and placed it on her breast.

"What do you say we have a few drinks here and then go back to my house?" she asked, her lips mere inches from his ear. "Or we can leave here now and have wine at my place."

He'd had women come on to him before, but never one quite so forward. Hell, she hadn't even bothered to share her name or ask for his. Even if Maddie weren't in his life, he'd pass on this woman's invitation.

Keith wrapped his fingers around her wrist and tugged her hand away. "I have a girlfriend."

Unfazed, the woman remained glued to his side. "I don't see her here with you now. And what she doesn't know won't hurt her. Trust me. We'll have fun."

"Not tonight." Keith released her wrist and moved as far away as he could without falling on his ass.

The woman's eyes darted toward the bar before settling on him again. "Well, if you change your mind, I'll be at the bar. But don't wait too long. You're not the only guy here alone tonight."

Keith watched her walk toward the bar. In the movies, guys wanted a wingman to pick up women. Tonight, he could've used one to help get rid of one. Whoever she was, Keith hoped she didn't come back.

HER COUSIN HATED to sit around at home. Nicole had been the only kid Lisa knew who hated watching television or playing video games. So it didn't surprise her when Nicole asked her to go out less than ten minutes after Lisa walked in the door. They'd settled on Murphy's because it was close and neither could come up with a better idea.

But now Lisa wondered if destiny hadn't played a role in their choice.

For days, she'd been racking her brain for a way to get some photos of Keith and Nicole together. She'd even reached out to Blake, a freelance photographer she'd known for years. If she found and hired someone who resembled Keith to do pictures with Nicole, Blake guaranteed he could manipulate the photo angles and lighting so Maddie believed the man with Nicole was Keith. And when Maddie questioned him about them, it would be his word against what was right in front of her eyes. Unfortunately, although Lisa knew a lot of men, none resembled Keith enough, and so far, she had found no one on the modeling sites Blake suggested.

Thanks to some perfect timing and her cousin's constant need to be anywhere but home, she no longer needed to worry about it.

Initially, she'd been confused when Nicole nudged her and announced it was her lucky day. Then she'd seen Keith walking toward the empty booth. The only other time she'd seen Keith in there alone had been the night he approached her at the bar. Fully aware this might be the only chance they got, Nicole didn't waste any time. As soon as the restaurant employee walked away, she'd moved in while Lisa immortalized the interaction in photos.

Retaking her spot at the bar, Nicole reached for her drink as Lisa scrolled through the photos she'd taken. "Did you get what you wanted?"

"Yep."

Now she just needed to decide which ones to send to Maddie. She'd started taking pictures as soon as Nicole sat down and hadn't stopped until her cousin stood up, so she had plenty to pick from. "What did you say to him?"

Not only was the place noisy, but she'd been too far away to hear Nicole and Keith's conversation.

"I invited him back to my house."

Lisa reached the most incriminating photo of the group and one she'd definitely be sending to Maddie. Although she'd known it was all an act, she'd wanted to walk over and drag her cousin away when Nicole placed Keith's hand over her breast.

"And since I'm sitting here with you, he turned me down," Nicole answered as the sound of a bird chirping came from her phone, alerting her to a message.

Nicole's answer didn't surprise her. Keith wasn't the type of guy to screw around behind someone's back. Guys like him preferred to just move on when they got bored with a woman. Or, as in their case, when he wasn't ready to admit he'd met the one. Soon Keith would come to his senses, though.

"Did he say anything about Maddie?"

"Only said he had a girlfriend."

Just because they hadn't arrived together didn't mean Keith wasn't meeting Maddie here. And if that were the plan, Lisa would have to put sending the pictures on hold. Thankfully, she could find out if Maddie was on her way there or not with a simple text.

Hey, I'm bored out of my mind. Do you want to grab some dinner and a drink?

After sending the message, Lisa gestured for the bartender to come over. Unfortunately, tonight, one Black and Gold would not be enough.

Next to her, Nicole stuffed her phone back into her tiny purse. "Shawn wants me to come by. So unless you want to call for a ride, we need to go."

Lisa wanted the second cocktail and the beef stew she'd been about to order. Unfortunately, she'd have to find another way home if she ordered either, because Nicole had driven tonight. While she took the occasional taxi or Uber, she avoided both whenever possible. At least Nicole was headed to Shawn's instead of the other way around, so she wouldn't hear them again tonight.

Accepting her credit card back, Lisa followed her cousin toward the entrance. "Thanks for your help tonight."

"You know I'm always there for you. But I still think you should move on. It's not like he's rich. And okay, I'll give you that he's good-looking, but he's no CJ Ferguson."

There weren't many men outside Hollywood who could compete with Lisa's favorite eye candy, actor CJ Ferguson. In her opinion, there weren't many in Hollywood that could either.

"Why didn't you tell me CJ is an option?"

Opening the car door, Nicole paused before getting inside. "If he were, I wouldn't be sharing the news with you."

"He'd pick me over you any day," Lisa said as she climbed into the car. "Hey, did you see CJ and Anderson Brady are doing another film together?" If anything would move Nicole's attention away from Keith, it was a conversation about their two favorite stars.

"No. What kind?"

"A romantic comedy. It's called *Island Love*."

A message from Maddie greeted her when she pulled out her beeping cell phone.

I would, but I'm in New York City.

The gods were really smiling down on her tonight.

Lucky. I love NYC. Have fun.

Smiling, Lisa put the device away. When she got home, she'd pick her favorite shots of Nicole and Keith and send them to Maddie. Hopefully, next week at this time, Keith would be with her instead of alone at Murphy's Tavern.

SEVEN

One thing you could say about Lady Haverston and her granddaughter, Violet, was that they didn't settle for anything less than the best. When the women flew, they went first class, and the cars they rode in cost as much as some small homes. Don't even get her started about the hotels they checked into. The three-bedroom suite they'd returned to tonight was larger than Maddie's first apartment. Far nicer too.

"My grandmother won't budge about staying longer." Violet dropped onto the sofa across from her.

Good.

Over the past six weeks, something close to a friendship had developed between Maddie and Violet. And it wasn't uncommon for them to chat about various topics, especially when Lady Haverston wasn't around. Maddie liked both women, and overall her time with them had been possibly the easiest assignment she'd had during her time with Elite Force. But she could only handle so many shopping trips, Broadway shows, and art exhibits—although, she wasn't sure some of what they saw could be called art.

Paintings and sculptures were not her thing. Still, Benjamin

Kress, who'd painted the pieces in the first exhibit they attended in California weeks ago, had been spectacular. Somehow, Kress had not only painted the models, but he'd captured their personalities. And Maddie understood why wealthy art collectors paid enormous sums for his work.

She couldn't say the same about the artwork they'd viewed last night. Maddie had received better paintings from her niece Phoebe, who was a kindergartener. She suspected interest in Camila Kegan's work had less to do with her talent, if you could call it that, and more to do with her last name. Grant Kegan, Camila's father, was the president of the New York Stock Exchange. Camila's grandfather, former Governor of New York Bob Kegan, was the current US Ambassador to the United Kingdom, and United States Congressman Ted Kegan was her uncle. If all those names weren't enough to catch people's attention, her uncle Jerry Kegan was one of the top ten movie producers in Hollywood, and her mom was the star of a popular long-running television drama. So yeah, Maddie would say the woman's popularity had more to do with who she knew than what she painted on canvases.

"Do you have to go back with your grandmother?"

They were both adults, so even though they'd arrived together, Maddie didn't see why Lady Haverston and Violet needed to leave together.

Violet leaned her head against her hand and sighed. "Unfortunately. Gran hates traveling alone. That's part of the reason I came with her. If I don't fly home with her on Friday, my dad won't be happy with me."

If Violet remained here, her grandmother wouldn't be doing much traveling alone. Friday morning, Maddie would accompany the countess to the airport and stay with her until she boarded the private plane they'd chartered to take them back to England. And Lady Haverston had no doubt arranged for someone to pick her up when she landed in London.

"My mom's not a fan of doing it either."

"Since I can't stay, Callie, my cousin's wife, offered to look at any places I'm interested in until I can come back."

Maddie didn't know why Violet felt it necessary to point out who she referred to. Even if she hadn't met the woman weeks ago, Maddie would know Callie was her cousin's wife. It'd been all the media could talk about when Violet's cousin, Dylan Talbot, married President Sherbrooke's daughter a few years ago.

"Hopefully, I can do that next month."

"You're thinking about moving here?"

New York City offered residents some things you wouldn't find anywhere else in the United States. Perhaps even the world. Still, the city ranked relatively low on her list of places she'd want to live. It was far too busy and crowded.

"At least for a little while," Violet answered. "Have you ever felt like you need a change but you're unsure what kind?"

Who hadn't? Most people, however, couldn't pick up and move to another country. "Not recently, but yes."

"I've felt that way for three or four months. Moving here feels right. My father won't see it that way, of course. And I might not tell him until after I've purchased something. But I'm still going to do it."

Maddie's parents weren't perfect, but they always supported her decisions. "Are you thinking house or condo?"

"Either. Callie's going to look at a brownstone I like on East 19th Street. It looks brilliant in the pictures." Picking up her cell phone, Violet brought up the real estate listing and then handed Maddie the device. "There's also a condo in Callie and Dylan's building that I'm interested in."

When they'd visited Dylan and his wife, they'd gone to their estate in Greenwich, Connecticut, where the couple spent most of their time rather than their New York City penthouse. But Maddie imagined the condos in their building looked nothing like the ones most people in the city called home.

Maddie scrolled through the listing. Built in 1855, both the pictures and the price tag took her breath away—not that she'd expected anything less. All real estate in New York City, regardless of the square footage and number of bedrooms, was crazy expensive. It was just another reason she'd never want to live there.

"It looks gorgeous."

No sooner did Maddie hand the device back than it rang. And after saying good night, Violet answered the call and disappeared into her bedroom.

Alone for the first time since she got dressed this morning, Maddie followed Violet's lead and headed to her room. Unless an emergency occurred, she wouldn't see either woman again tonight. So rather than switch on the television, she dug out her e-reader and headed into the bathroom so she could take advantage of the hot tub in there. Much like the full kitchen, the private bathrooms attached to each bedroom were just one of the hotel suite's many luxuries.

Once submerged in the warm, bubbling water, she turned on the e-reader and returned to perhaps her all-time favorite novel. One she owned both paperback and digital versions of, and she'd read so many times she now skimmed over those scenes she deemed irrelevant. And no matter how many times she read it, Maddie loved the scene where the hero and heroine saw each other for the first time in five years. As she read, Maddie could imagine the young knight walking into the castle's family chapel and seeing the woman he'd loved for years kneeling in front of a saint and praying.

Just as the heroine turned, expecting to see the knight's younger brother, Maddie's cell phone interrupted the silence and pulled her out of the story.

Groaning, Maddie dropped her head back and considered ignoring the text message until she was ready to get out. Since Ax knew she was out of state with the countess and her granddaughter and wouldn't be back until tomorrow, the message probably wasn't from him. Except for Lisa, who'd sent her a message earlier, her friends didn't know she was out of town, so it could be one of them wanting to grab a late dinner. But if she didn't get back to them right away, they'd assume she was busy and go about their evening. Then again, it could be Keith. She hadn't heard from him since Monday. He'd left her a short voice mail letting her know he was headed to Miami on a kidnapping case.

The phone beeped again. "Yeah, I heard you the first time."

Whoever had decided people needed a reminder that they'd received a text should be fired. No one wanted an electronic device shouting at them when they didn't jump to do its bidding the moment it made a sound.

Instead of finding a message from Keith, Maddie found another one from Lisa when she unlocked the phone.

Hey, Maddie. I'm at Murphy's.

I got out of the hot tub for that. She looked back at the relaxing water.

Have fun.

What else could she write and not sound rude?

I think Keith's here.

So? Keith often stopped at the restaurant. If he was there now, it just meant he was back from Florida. Most likely, he went over for dinner or to pick up some takeout. It wasn't like the guy was much of a cook unless it involved a grill or a microwave.

Is this him?

A photo featuring either Keith or an identical twin he'd failed to tell her about cozied up with a blonde appeared on her screen.

She'd read about characters seeing red. But, until now, she'd never experienced it.

A second photo followed the first, and Maddie sat down on the toilet seat cover. Keith's hand covered the woman's breast in this one, and her lips were mere inches away from his ear.

No. The guy in the picture was not Keith. He just looked like him. Yep, if she closed her eyes and counted to ten, when she looked at the picture again, she'd realize the two men just shared a resemblance. Keith wasn't at Murphy's with some woman glued to his side. He was in Florida working on a kidnapping assignment.

Her phone beeped again just as she reached the number ten.

Are you still there?

Yeah. That looks like Keith.

It can't be, though. Keith left relationships when he got bored. He didn't cheat, the part of her brain not consumed with anger pointed out. Just as quickly, though, it reminded her of the obvious. Pictures didn't lie. And the person at Murphy's sure as hell appeared to be Keith.

Lisa's next message appeared almost immediately.

Do you want me to go over and say something to him?

If it were Keith, he'd be more likely to leave than cause a scene. It was anyone's guess how the blonde would react. Lisa might find herself in an even uglier situation if it turned out it wasn't Keith but some random guy.

No. I'll call him.

And I better like his answers.

If you need to talk later, call me. Doesn't matter the time. Thanks.

She appreciated the offer, but regardless of what Keith said, she wouldn't be taking Lisa up on the offer.

What she wore made no difference. But she exchanged the bath towel for her pajamas before pulling up Keith's number, anyway.

Reaching the bedroom door, Maddie turned and retraced her steps as the phone rang. "Answer the phone, Keith."

"Hey, are you done with babysitting duty for the night?" Keith asked, and she could hear the smile in his voice.

Rather than ease her anger, his friendly greeting sent it up a notch. A guy who was getting up close and personal with another woman shouldn't sound so relaxed when his girlfriend called.

Her grip on the phone tightened as she concentrated on not clenching her jaw. "Everyone's tucked in."

Don't accuse him of anything.

"What about you? Are you still in Florida?" If he said yes, Maddie could call Alex for confirmation, because she'd also been part of the team Elite Force sent down there.

"Got back earlier today. I'm over at Murphy's with Alex and Spike."

Maddie forgot about not clenching her teeth, and she actually felt her nostrils flare.

Sure you are.

If Keith were with Alex and Spike, he wouldn't have his hand on another woman. If he even tried it, they'd call him out and then make sure she knew.

"So that's the story you're going with." She heard the anger in her voice. While she'd rather sound indifferent, she preferred to sound angry instead of hurt.

"It's the truth. After the debrief, we met here," Keith replied, confusion clear in his voice.

He's good. Maddie would give him that.

"I have some pictures that are telling me something else, Keith. Why don't you check them out and then try again?" she said before forwarding the two photos to him. So much for not accusing him of anything. But hey, she was only human. She didn't wait for a response before continuing. "Because the person sitting next to you doesn't look like Spike to me."

ALEX WAS NEXT TO HIM, while Spike sat across the table. Not that it mattered, because it didn't help clarify Maddie's comments. If she were at home, he'd ask if she had been drinking. That was how much sense she was making.

With no idea of what he'd see, Keith lowered his phone. A photo of him with his hand on the blonde's breast and one of her all but sitting in his lap greeted him.

"Who sent you these?"

Half a second after speaking the words, Keith realized his mistake. The question made him sound guilty. And dammit, he'd done nothing wrong. The woman had sat down next to him. He hadn't invited her.

"A friend. So you don't deny that it's you in those pictures?"

I wish I could.

Keith scanned the crowd. He didn't see any of her friends, but he didn't know all of them either. But someone in here not only recognized him but took photos without his permission. Photos that didn't tell the complete story.

Up to that point, Alex and Spike had been arguing about which was better: ice cream or frozen custard. It was a stupid argument, because everyone knew ice cream was superior. But both shut up and focused on him when he said, "No, but I don't know who she is."

"Then you make a habit of groping women you don't know." Maddie's tone went from angry to furious.

Dragging his hand across his face, he wished a slow and agonizing death to the blonde and whoever had sent Maddie the pictures.

"Maddie, you know me better than that. And it's not what it looks like. The woman in the photo sat down next to me while I waited for Alex and Spike. She put my hand there and invited me back to her house."

Several surveillance cameras recorded everything that happened in the restaurant, so there was a good chance one had recorded the whole encounter. Too bad he had no way to access the data.

"When I turned her down, she left and returned to the bar. That's it. About five minutes later, Alex and Spike got here. We've been together ever since."

"Some random woman just sat down, placed your hand on her boob, and invited you back to her house?" Skepticism dripped from Maddie's voice.

It sounded like an unlikely scenario, even to him. However, that didn't change the fact that it had happened.

He'd never cheated on a girlfriend and certainly didn't intend to start now. But if he'd planned to take a woman home with him while Maddie was away, he wouldn't do it while waiting for their friends to show up. "Do you honestly think I would've invited her over while waiting for Spike and Alex?"

"They're with you now?"

Isn't that what I just said?

People could call him a lot of names. Liar wasn't one of them. Maddie knew that. Or at least she should after all the time they'd spent together as first coworkers and now lovers.

"Talk to Alex yourself." Pissed, he didn't wait for a response. Instead, he handed Alex the phone.

"Hey, Maddie," Alex said as she slipped out of the booth.

Across from him, Spike rested his forearms on the table and leaned forward. "Let me see if I've got this right. One of Maddie's friends took a picture of you with another woman and then sent it to her."

Nodding, Keith drained the last of his beer and glanced around for their server.

"And you don't know who she was?"

"You were sitting right here when I said that. Maybe you need to get your hearing checked," Keith answered as he caught Junior's eye and gestured for him to come over.

"Yeah, I know what you told Maddie. But I thought maybe the woman was someone you'd gone out with in the past looking to get back together, and you modified the story a little."

"Tonight was the first time I ever saw the damn woman." And he hoped never to see her again.

"What can I get for you?" Junior asked, stopping by the table and putting a temporary halt to their conversation. Spike's expression promised that he'd go back to interrogating Keith the moment the guy left, though.

I should've gone the fuck home tonight.

"Another beer."

"Why don't you bring us all another round," Spike said before Junior could ask if he wanted anything.

As Keith expected, Spike didn't waste any time once the employee left. "Did Maddie tell you who sent her the pictures?"

He had seen none of her friends while on the phone with Maddie and didn't expect to see any now. Still, he looked toward the crowded bar. "No."

Alex slid into the booth next to him and handed him his phone. "I think you're good."

You think?

He'd done nothing other than be in the wrong place at the wrong time.

"Maddie."

"Hey, I, uh, I'm sorry. I should've believed you. Those pictures, well, they got to me."

He didn't like it, but his first reaction would've been similar if a buddy had sent him photos of Maddie with another guy. Initially anyway. Common sense would've moved in once the shock wore off, because he trusted Maddie. At least, that was the story he planned to tell himself. He didn't want to find out what his actual reaction would've been.

"I get it. Let's forget it happened." As much as he wanted to know which of her friends was to blame, he wouldn't ask Maddie again.

"Yeah. Let's do that. I'll see you tomorrow."

Ending the call, Keith set the device down next to his beer and nudged Alex in the ribs. "Did she tell you who sent the pictures?"

Even though it wouldn't change anything, Keith wanted to know who'd stuck their nose where it didn't belong.

Alex shook her head and popped a fry into her mouth. "But I didn't ask either. Does it matter?"

"Maybe." Spike didn't wait for Keith to ask what he meant by that comment. "It seems too convenient that someone Maddie knows was here at just the right time to see a woman you've never met join you."

"It's called a coincidence." Or plain old bad luck.

"I'm not sure I buy that," Spike replied.

Keith wasn't sure he wanted to know, but he'd ask. "Oh, wise one, what's your theory?"

"The two women were working together. Maybe Maddie's friend wants her to boot your ass for some reason. She could also be the one who sent you those texts."

He'd heard his friend say some stupid things, but this topped the list. "You're crazy."

"We already knew that about him. But Spike makes a good point." Alex's statement proved his belief that nothing good ever followed the word "but" in a sentence.

"I'm not going to repeat Jasmine's words, but she once went into great detail about how she wanted to spend time with you."

Keith didn't get how Alex could swear like a drunk pirate, but when it came to discussing sex, she acted like a nun at a convent.

"And Maddie said Cassidy wouldn't leave you alone a few months ago," Alex added as Junior returned and placed three beers on the table.

Yeah, he remembered the night Alex referred to, but he still thought Spike's theory was bullshit. "Not buying it. Neither of them would do that to Maddie. They've been friends for too long. And other than the two of you and Matt, no one knew I'd be here tonight."

Unless you were tailing a person, it was damn tricky to set someone up when you didn't know where they would be in advance.

Spike shrugged as he raised his beer toward his mouth. "Maybe, but something about tonight feels..." He paused. "Manipulated. I'd watch my back if I were you."

He was going to buy Spike a dictionary for his birthday so the guy could look up the word "coincidence."

EIGHT

MADDIE WATCHED THE CHILDREN PLAYING NEAR THE WATER'S EDGE and the waves crashing on the beach as the sound of a fighter jet filled the air. A moment later, the children disappeared, and Jimi Hendrix appeared suspended over the sand with his guitar. Soon, his voice and music drowned out all other sounds. Mesmerized, she watched his fingers dance over the guitar strings. But why was he here, and how could he remain in the air like that?

As a wave crashed on the beach, Keith and a blonde wearing a bright red bikini appeared, holding hands and walking along the sand. When they reached a sandcastle, he put his hand on her breast like in the photo as she whispered in his ear. Then, just as suddenly as the couple appeared, they and Jimi Hendrix began to fade. Somehow, though, she could still hear his music. She didn't remember the song's name, but she'd heard it before. Keith often played the man's music in his truck.

Thud. Maddie's head bounced off the truck window, and the beach instantly disappeared. Opening her eyes, she shifted in her seat as the song Hendrix sang in her dream continued to come through the truck's speakers.

Explains why the man was in my dream.

As for the appearance of Keith with another woman, well,

she'd had similar dreams ever since Lisa sent her those photos. Each time it happened, or she thought about the pictures, a weird combination of anger and regret bombarded Maddie. Not surprisingly, the anger was directed toward the blonde who'd come on to Keith. Who did the woman think she was?

Maddie's lack of trust in Keith caused her feelings of regret. For over a year and a half, they'd worked dangerous assignments where they depended on each other to remain safe. Keith wouldn't betray her trust by cheating when he knew, tomorrow, she might be the only thing standing between him and a trip to the hospital or worse—just one fact Alex had reminded her of on Tuesday night. And one she would've eventually remembered when the shock of seeing Keith with the woman—who Alex had referred to as a floozy—wore off.

"Have a nice nap?" Keith glanced in her direction briefly before focusing on the road again.

She'd closed her eyes because of a headache, not so she could take a nap. "Well, my headache is gone." But, unfortunately, a cramp in her neck had replaced it. It was bound to happen when you fell asleep with your head resting on a truck window. "I'm sorry. I didn't mean to fall asleep. How long was I out?"

Yesterday they'd caught a late-afternoon flight out of Dulles airport. After landing at TF Green, which, according to Keith, was in Warwick, not Providence as everyone always claimed, they'd driven straight to his parents' house. There she'd been greeted by not only Reggie and Erica Wallace at dinner but also Keith's two sisters, his brother-in-law, Dan, and his niece, Bella. Then, not long after a late breakfast this morning, they'd hopped on Interstate 95 toward Maine. However, she remembered seeing the sign stating they were crossing into New Hampshire, so she'd fallen asleep sometime between then and now.

"About an hour. It's probably a good thing you got some rest now." The car in front of them stopped when the traffic light turned yellow, leaving Keith no other choice but to do the same.

"You won't be getting much rest tonight." The glint in Keith's eyes as he smiled was guaranteed to melt any woman with a pulse. Maddie included.

If he'd told her how long the drive from his parents' house to their hotel in Maine would take, Maddie didn't remember. "Are we almost there?"

If they'd be there soon, she could wait. Otherwise, she needed Keith to find her a bathroom.

"About another ten minutes."

If it meant not using a public restroom, she could wait another ten minutes.

"But I was going to stop at Marginal Way and then the market. I want to pick up some wine and snacks for the room."

Maddie often did the same when on vacation, so she didn't spend a fortune eating out or on room service. And she was curious about Marginal Way. Both Keith's mom and his sister had mentioned the location last night when they learned Maddie had never been to Maine.

"Can we check in and then go do that?"

"Whatever you want."

Roughly ten minutes later, Keith turned into the parking lot for the Admiral's Resort. Unlike more traditional hotels, the resort consisted of five four-story buildings, four of which appeared to be connected. With fall upon them, the owners had decorated the grounds with pumpkins, mums, and the biggest scarecrow she'd ever seen.

The fall-themed decorations didn't end at the main entrance. Orange and burgundy mums that were reminiscent of the fall foliage outside added color to the lobby. A cornucopia filled with mini pumpkins, different types of squashes, and colorful leaves sat on the mantel over the fireplace.

"Your suite is in the Sebago Wing. Just follow this hallway to the end and take a right." The hotel employee at the registration desk gestured toward the hallway running past the fireplace. "Our indoor pool and the Roman bath are both open from seven in the morning until ten at night. The fitness room has the same hours, and it's located in the basement of the Echo Wing. You will need your room key to access it."

Maddie could see the indoor pool. Like most indoor hotel pools, it was much smaller than the one she'd noticed outside. Fully enclosed in glass, the area currently being used by a couple with two children appeared inviting. Later tonight, she wouldn't mind coming down for a swim, especially if they had the area to themselves. Unfortunately, there was no sign of the Roman bath the employee mentioned, and she wondered what they'd find there.

"Since it is the off-season, Acadia only serves dinner. There should be a menu in your suite. The restaurant provides room service. You should also find a map of the area in your suite." After inserting two room keys into a holder, the employee handed it to Keith. "If you need anything, please don't hesitate to call the front desk. Enjoy your stay."

Maddie waited until they were down the hall before speaking. "Echo and Sebago are interesting names for a hotel to use."

"The owners named all the wings after lakes in Maine. And in case you couldn't guess, the restaurant takes its name from the national park further north."

She'd assumed that. Even though she'd never spent time in the state, she'd heard of Acadia National Park. "You've stayed here before?"

Keith had insisted on not only making their hotel reservations but also paying for their stay. Finally, she'd given in after he reminded her they were only traveling here this weekend so he could attend his friend's wedding.

"Three or four times. But my parents always stay either here or at Seabrook By The Sea. I tried to book something there because it overlooks the ocean, but they didn't have any suites available this weekend."

A standard room would've sufficed since they were staying

only two nights. But hey, it was Keith's money. He could spend it any way he wanted.

When they reached the end of the hall, they turned right. But before they reached the elevator, Keith stopped next to a glass door.

"That's the Roman bath. We can come down later and check it out if you want."

Maddie paused near the glass door long enough to peek inside. At the moment, two guests occupied the large whirlpool with waterfalls situated in the center of the room. Lounge chairs lined the walls, and various indoor plants brought nature inside. Floor-to-ceiling windows along the outermost wall gave the room's occupants a pleasant view of a flower garden. In one corner, there was a sauna, and a steam room in the other completed the room.

"Sounds like a great idea to me."

It didn't matter if it was the tub in her bathroom or an indoor hotel pool. Something about being in the water always relaxed her. Since this was a mini vacation for her, relaxation was a top priority.

When the elevator doors opened, they stepped inside, and Keith pressed the button for the fourth floor.

"Or we can use the hot tub in our suite and not worry about bathing suits," Keith said, putting his arm across her shoulders and kissing her cheek.

There was nothing quite like sex while submerged in water, and they couldn't do that in the Roman bath or the hotel pool. Well, technically, they could, but they'd risk getting kicked out of the hotel and possibly arrested. Maddie enjoyed seeing new places, but the inside of a jail cell wasn't one of them.

"I like that idea even more."

The elevator doors opened, and Maddie stepped into a foyer with a hallway leading off to the left. "Now that is art," she said.

A sculpture of a young girl rested in the center of a dark green, circular sofa. With her arms raised and braids flying behind her, it appeared as though she was running through the waves crashing over her feet. According to the small plaque nestled among the flowers planted around the sculpture, the piece was called *Dancing In The Waves*.

Not quite halfway down the hall, Keith stopped in front of a door marked 406. "Didn't like what you saw in New York?" he asked, placing his card near the door lock and turning the handle.

Besides saying she was glad to be home, Maddie hadn't talked about her most recent trip to the Big Apple.

"You could probably paint something better than what I saw." Maddie preceded Keith into the suite as soon as he opened the door and made a beeline for the bathroom.

When she emerged, Keith stepped back inside and closed one of the sliding glass doors that led to their private balcony. While not as luxurious as the suites she'd stayed in with the countess and her granddaughter, it was a hundred times nicer than what one would find at one of the many roadside motels they'd passed on the way here. It was also far nicer than anything she would've booked for herself.

The king-sized bed faced the sliding glass doors and a small table with two chairs. A vase of long-stemmed roses, an unopened bottle of champagne, two wineglasses, and a box of chocolates currently occupied the table. All of which Keith must have arranged beforehand because Maddie doubted the hotel left the items in every room. The decorators had positioned two armchairs near the gas fireplace at the far end of the suite. A two-person hot tub occupied the corner opposite from the fireplace, allowing guests to watch the flames while soaking. Assuming they weren't occupied by other things, of course. And without a doubt, later, they would find themselves in it, with the fireplace on while drinking champagne. Maybe or maybe not eating the chocolates.

"Remind me to have you book all my getaways."

Maddie picked up the silver box with the name Favre printed on the side. Made in Europe and only recently sold in the US, she'd only had chocolate from the company once, and that had been while in France.

"Let me guess, these are for you, and the flowers are for me?" She'd always believed she had an unhealthy love of chocolate. Then she met Keith, and he proved her wrong.

After taking the box and setting it back down, Keith wrapped his arms around her waist. "I might be willing to give you a piece. Maybe even two, if you ask nicely."

"Then maybe I'll let you have half a glass of champagne. A whole one, if you ask nicely."

A smile tugged at the corners of Keith's mouth. "Who said the champagne is for you? Maybe that and the chocolates have my name on them."

"Well, I'll get my own and bring it back in that case. Same with the chocolates."

Pulling her closer to him, he kissed her forehead. "All three are for you." He brushed his lips across hers. "But if you want to share the chocolate, that would be great."

She'd never pegged Keith as the romantic type. The evidence around her suggested she'd been wrong. "I'll think about it. But just in case, pick up some when we go to the store."

SINCE TODAY WAS a picture-perfect fall day, something they wouldn't get too many more of, they opted to walk to Marginal Way rather than drive. And roughly fifteen minutes after leaving their hotel, Keith and Maddie approached Shore Road and one of the cliff walk's two entrances.

He'd once read an article about Ogunquit in some travel magazine while in the doctor's waiting room. In it, the author referred to Marginal Way—which connected Perkins Cove to Ogunquit Beach and was one of the few paved public shoreline paths in New England—as a gorgeous tightrope strung along the Atlantic Ocean.

Keith had to agree. Whenever he came to the area, he walked the path regardless of the weather. Others might disagree, but he found the ocean mesmerizing even during a rainstorm or below-zero temperature.

"Dogs are only allowed during certain times of the year," Maddie said, pausing to read a sign posted at the start of the path, listing all the things prohibited from the area.

Along with scooters, skateboards, rollerblades, and bicycles, it stated that no dogs were allowed between April and September —not that everyone followed the rule. Sometimes they got away with it. Other times, they found themselves slapped with a nice little fine.

"Why is it okay the rest of the year but not then?" she asked.

Although a cool, late-October afternoon, numerous people enjoyed the walk and views. And during the warmer months, it wasn't unusual to see four or five times as many people of all ages there.

Keith took her hand and waited for a couple with a stroller to exit the path before entering. "My guess is because those months are tourist season around here. People from all over pack this area in the spring and summer."

"That makes sense. So how long is this path?"

He'd never looked it up, but he'd always been good at estimating distances. "I'd say it's a little over a mile from here to the end. But if you get tired, there are benches all along the way where we can rest."

He couldn't resist adding the last part. Keith had seen Maddie run up to ten miles on the treadmill, so this walk would be a piece of cake for her.

"It might be tough, but I think I'll make it. But hey, if you need a break, just say the word."

Neither spoke again as they made their way along the walkway. Instead, Keith enjoyed the sound of the waves crashing below, the rustling leaves, and the feel of Maddie's hand in his.

"It must cost a fortune to stay there in the summer," Maddie said, pointing to a hotel on their left as they passed by it.

With only a fence and gate separating the property from the walkway, the Seabrook By The Sea Hotel was one of the nicest resorts in the area. Over the years, he'd passed the area more than once and seen couples getting married on the sprawling green lawn between the wrought-iron fence and the main building.

"Yep, and you have to book months in advance or forget about getting a room."

Keith moved to the left so the jogger coming toward them could pass on his right. It wasn't uncommon to see joggers here. However, he'd always thought they were missing out on all the beauty around them by running instead of taking a stroll.

"The wedding is there tomorrow. Colby mentioned a lot of the guests are staying there. That's probably why I couldn't book what I wanted."

"It's a beautiful spot for an outdoor wedding. Is the wedding outside?" Maddie asked, glancing over her shoulder at the resort.

Colby hadn't given him any details other than where and when to be there. "No idea. I guess we'll find out today."

"What time is the rehearsal dinner tonight?"

"Five. But there is no dinner involved."

After rounding a bend in the path, Maddie stopped short, forcing him to either stop or pull her along behind him. "You're kidding. Isn't it a tradition to practice for the wedding and then afterward for the wedding party to have dinner together?"

He'd been part of two other weddings, and both times the night before the big day, he attended events similar to what Maddie described. "Maybe, but Colby does things his way. We're going to run through things, and then we're on our own."

The view from the bench next to them was too good to pass up. So, although he didn't need a rest, Keith moved closer and sat down before someone else scooped it up.

"When it's over, I thought we could get dinner at the Maine

Lobster Pound." He might have spent the first twelve years of his life living first on an army base in Texas and then in Washington, but he loved seafood as much as any native New Englander. And a person wouldn't find anything better than Maine seafood.

"That depends. Does it serve anything other than lobster? Because if they don't, you either need to think of another place, or we'll order room service."

"They do. Not a lobster fan?" Keith liked lobster, but he didn't love it.

Maddie shrugged. "I've never tried it, and I don't plan to."

"Why's that?"

While on a security detail with her in Oklahoma, he'd seen Maddie try fried rattlesnake. She'd been the only one on the three-person team to try it. So she wasn't squeamish when it came to food.

"They drop the poor things in boiling water alive, Keith. I don't care if they taste good or not. That's just cruel."

She wasn't wrong. And on the rare occasion Keith did order lobster, he didn't think about how the restaurant cooked them. "I'm thinking cod or salmon sounds good for dinner."

A couple who had to be pushing their mid-seventies stopped close to them. "Excuse me," the woman said, temporarily halting their conversation. "Would you mind taking a picture of us together?"

"Of course not." Standing, Maddie accepted the woman's cell phone.

After sticking his Retired Air Force Veteran baseball hat in his back pocket, the man put his arm around the woman's shoulders.

Keith rarely thought too far into the future. And when he did, those thoughts didn't include a wife. But just then, instead of seeing the older couple, Keith pictured him and Maddie standing in the same spot in forty years or so and asking a younger couple to snap some photos.

"We came here on our honeymoon fifty years ago today. I have a picture of us in about the same spot hanging on our wall," the woman explained, accepting her phone back. "I'm going to put this one next to it."

Fifty years with the same person.

A year ago, he would've said it wasn't in his future. Today, it sounded possible.

"By the way, I'm Barbara, and this is my husband, John."

Much like how some people insisted on hugging when they greeted you, he'd never understood why some people felt compelled to give you their name when you'd never see them again.

"It's nice to meet you both. I'm Maddie, and this is Keith."

"Would you like me to take one of you together?" Barbara asked.

They didn't have any pictures together, and this was a beautiful spot. "That'd be great," Keith answered.

Like Maddie had done, the woman took several photos before handing the device back and walking away.

Instead of taking her hand, Keith put his arm around Maddie's shoulders as they continued their walk toward Perkins Cove.

"I love the water. And if we were in the Caribbean or even Florida, I'd go for a swim. But no way would you get me in it around here today." Maddie pointed toward the handful of surfers and divers below.

"If I had a wetsuit with me, I'd go in a heartbeat. There's nothing quite like the ocean. It's one of my favorite places to be."

"If you feel that way, why didn't you join the navy?"

"My great-grandfather enlisted in the army after high school, and my dad joined after college. And my grandfather went to West Point. They would've kicked me out of the family if I had joined the navy."

"Somehow, I doubt that."

"You've never seen them during the army/navy football game." Keith had learned many of the more colorful words in his vocabulary while spending time with the three men as they watched the games.

"Sounds like my dad when he's watching college basketball, especially if Virginia Tech is playing. Tucker is the only person who'll watch those games with him."

He'd never understood some people's obsession with college basketball—or basketball in general, for that matter. Keith enjoyed a pickup game with friends. However, he couldn't handle sitting in front of the television and watching players run up and down the court. Football, especially at the college level, was another matter. And he occasionally stayed home on a Saturday and watched every game he could tune in to.

"Does he live close to your parents?"

Maddie's parents lived in the Virginia Beach area, and now Spencer lived close to her. But he didn't know where her older brother or younger sister called home.

"Tucker and his family live in Cape Charles, so they're about an hour away from my parents, depending on traffic. But Autumn is only ten or fifteen minutes away from them. I think she spends more time at their house than her apartment."

Maddie navigated them around a four-or-five-year-old kid having a meltdown because his parents wouldn't let him climb down the rocks and touch the water. Keith couldn't blame the kid for wanting to go down there. The water looked inviting.

"I know you've never met Autumn, but did you meet Tucker and his wife when they visited in January?"

"Nope. I was escorting Stan Bond's sorry ass on one of his Venezuelan trips."

A bigmouth oil guy from Texas, Stan frequently hired Elite Force to keep him safe when he traveled outside the country. The guy had made eight trips to Venezuela in the past ten months. Unfortunately, Keith had accompanied him four times, and he knew the man wasn't traveling there for business, which explained why his wife had never traveled with him.

"Please don't remind me of him. The seaweed in the ocean here has more class than him." Maddie had landed the undesirable assignment in April.

To hell with the seaweed. The rocks on the shore had more class than Bond. Mega wealthy client or not, Keith hoped the guy took his business elsewhere the next time he traveled south of the border.

"Anyway, Tucker invited us over for Thanksgiving. It's his and Brittany's turn to host. My parents and my grandparents will be there too. Brittany's parents always go to her brother's house, so you don't have to worry about them." A hint of uncertainty lurked in her voice. "I told him I needed to check with you."

Mom wanted him home for the holiday. However, after Keith told her he planned to spend Thanksgiving with Maddie and her family, she wouldn't complain. She'd been dropping subtle hints since his niece was born about him getting into a serious relationship.

"What do you think?" she asked.

Honestly, he'd hoped to spend Thanksgiving with his family this year. Thanks to work, he hadn't been able to make it last November. But he wanted to spend the holiday with Maddie more, even if it meant going to her brother's house.

"I'm good with whatever you want to do."

NINE

Before this evening, Maddie had attended two wedding rehearsals. The first was when her older brother got married. Rather than get married locally, Tucker and Brittany had opted for a destination wedding. The entire wedding party and many of the guests had arrived in Aruba well before the ceremony. Much like the wedding, only one word described the rehearsal dinner, which had capped off several days of events: Lavish. The second one had been for her college roommate's wedding. That night, following several run-throughs at the church, everyone gathered inside one of Ciao Bella's private function rooms for dinner. While both events had similarities, each couple had put their own stamp on things. The same was true about Colby and Amari's rehearsal tonight.

After doing a single practice run for the next day, both sets of parents headed out to dinner together. Amari's brother, his girlfriend, and the wedding party, which consisted of only Keith and the maid of honor, went to the resort's bar for a round of drinks with the bride and groom. Less than twenty minutes later, the maid of honor and her boyfriend left. Amari's brother and his girlfriend followed shortly after, leaving Keith and Maddie alone with the future bride and groom.

"Hey, are you going to be around for Thanksgiving?" Colby asked, placing his empty beer glass down.

"We're spending it with Maddie's family."

Maddie had received her sister-in-law's invitation earlier in the week. Since they hadn't talked about it, she hadn't known what Keith's plans were or even if he wanted to spend the holiday with her. Rather than accept or decline, she filled Brittany in on her relationship status, because even though Maddie didn't think her sister-in-law would mind if she brought a date, it'd be beyond rude for her to show with a surprise guest in tow. As she expected, Brittany had assured her Keith was welcome too if Maddie decided to come. Even though she'd received a green light to bring a guest, she had not asked Keith until today.

To say she'd been uncertain about how Keith would respond to her invitation was an understatement. In college, she'd learned that some guys could be weird when it came to spending the holidays with their moms. She'd dated Richard for eight months during her sophomore year. He'd insisted on spending every holiday with the woman, including St. Patrick's Day. And whenever his mom called asking Richard to come home, he went, even when they had plans. It'd been the primary reason Maddie ended their relationship, because while she understood Richard wanting to be there for his mom, she didn't want to always come in second to the woman.

She knew Keith wasn't a stereotypical momma's boy like Richard, but that didn't mean he wouldn't prefer to spend the upcoming holiday with his family, especially since he hadn't been able to last year.

Colby's eyebrows rose ever so slightly at Keith's answer. "We won't be around in December, but you'll have to stop by the next time you're up. I finished the room over the garage, and the pool table is being delivered next week."

Earlier, Amari had shared that the couple was having a traditional Hindu wedding in December. So right after Thanksgiving, the couple was leaving for India, where Amari had been born, and all her family except her parents and brother lived.

"Sounds good." Keith took the last sip from his glass and set it down next to her empty one. "Unless you two have plans, how about another round, and then we go to dinner?"

On the way over to the resort, she'd suggested Keith invite Colby and his fiancée to dinner with them. Today was the first time Keith had seen his friend in months, and who knew how long it'd be before he got another chance?

"Depends. Are you buying?" Colby asked, reminding her of her brother Spencer. The guy never passed up a free meal or drink.

Keith nodded. "But only because it's the night before your wedding."

"In that case, I'll have two more beers before we go."

"You're only getting one."

"Maddie, what did you have?" Amari asked, grabbing the cocktail menu as their server approached the table. "I want to try something new."

When Maddie traveled, she liked to try drinks unique to the area. So before ordering, she'd searched the drink menu for something she'd never had before but might enjoy.

"A Maine cosmo. It was good, especially if you like coffee." Unlike a traditional cosmo, this one included coffee brandy made at a company located in Maine. "I'm going to have another." Then, if the restaurant had any signature drinks at dinner, she might try something else.

Amari set the cocktail menu aside. "I love coffee. I'll try one of those."

"Hey, did you see that David Nelson is playing for the Rebels this year?" Keith asked once they'd ordered another round of drinks. Then, glancing her way, he added, "The three of us played football together at URI."

After providing her with the information, Keith and Colby's conversation turned to football. As far as professional sports went, football ranked near the bottom of her list, so not only did she not recognize the player's name, she didn't care about how his season or the team's was going so far. Now, if they'd been talking about baseball, it'd be a different story.

"Colby mentioned you and Keith work together," Amari said while Colby and Keith debated who was a better running back, their former college teammate, Junior Morris, another New England player, or Zach Ferdinand, who'd left the Rebels and now played for Green Bay.

While she hadn't recognized David's name and had never heard of Zach Ferdinand, she recognized the name Junior Morris. Perhaps one of the most handsome guys in the NFL, he appeared in commercials and billboard ads for various products. And if his football career ended tomorrow, Junior could quickly start working in Hollywood.

Maddie nodded. "It's where we met."

Other than for a short time during the wedding rehearsal, she hadn't left Keith's side all night. So unless Keith had mentioned her before tonight, she didn't know when he could've shared the information.

"Colby and I do too."

"Is that how you two met?"

Just because they worked together didn't mean that was where they'd met. Some companies employed so many people that an individual could spend their entire career there and still not meet everyone. So, while it was possible that they had cubicles next to each other, or they'd met in the elevator, it was also possible that a mutual coworker had introduced them.

Amari shook her head as she sipped her drink. "Believe it or not, we had a few classes together in college. Colby and Keith even lived on the floor above me during our freshman year. After that, I didn't see him again until three years ago, when I started working for Epic Gaming. At the time, our cubicles were next to each other. He asked me out my first week there. If I'd been smart, I would've gone out with him then."

The next day they were getting married, so she'd agreed at some point. "Dating coworkers can make things complicated."

"Sometimes. But I didn't turn him down because we worked together. When Colby asked, I had a boyfriend. Someone I stayed with far longer than I should have. Wesley hated that Colby and I were friends. He didn't like me being friends with men at all, but Colby bothered him the most."

Everyone got jealous occasionally. And anyone who told you differently was lying. However, any relationship was doomed if one party suffered from constant jealousy and distrust.

"When I broke up with Wesley about a year ago, I wanted to pursue things with Colby. But, of course, by then, he was seeing someone." Amari paused and checked her ringing cell phone. Either she didn't recognize the number or it wasn't important because she declined the call before setting it down and taking another sip of her drink.

"Then, about two and a half months ago, we attended a programming convention in San Diego together for work, and on our first night there, he asked me to dinner. We haven't spent a day apart since."

She'd have to fill Keith in on the couple's backstory when they got back to the hotel. Maybe then he'd have fewer reservations about their marriage.

A LARGE SIGN with a red lobster and the words "Maine Lobster Pound and Steakhouse" painted on it welcomed Maddie and Keith when he pulled into the parking lot behind Amari and Colby's car a short while later.

"Looks a bit like a log cabin," Maddie said before opening the car door.

The building's exterior reminded Maddie of her dad's old Lincoln logs that she'd played with as a kid at her grandparents' house. The same set her grandparents passed on to Dad when they'd moved into a retirement community, and now her niece used them when she visited Maddie's parents.

"Yeah, I've always thought that too."

A paved walkway led from the parking lot to the restaurant's front entrance. A flagstone fireplace dominated the lawn. Someone had placed colorful Adirondack chairs on the grass and along the walkway's edge so people could sit while waiting for a table inside.

All the chairs were empty tonight, but there was a nice blaze going in the fireplace. If anyone sat outside while they waited for a table to open up, they wouldn't have to worry about being chilly.

Although not typical for a restaurant to have an outside fire going, it wasn't what Maddie found so unique about the place. Nope, that award went to the roof, jutting out from the building and covering what looked like an open porch near the entrance. From the parking lot, at least, it looked like it'd make a perfect spot for guests to sit outside to eat. A small outside bar might work well there too. However, there weren't any tables or even a bar underneath the roof.

Instead, a sizeable, rectangular-shaped object with concrete sides sat in the middle of the space while four employees wearing red T-shirts and aprons stood around talking to each other.

Maddie gestured toward the area before following Amari into the building. "What's all that about?"

"They keep the lobsters in the tank there. If you order one for dinner, you go over and pick out the one you want. Then it's cooked and delivered to the table," Keith answered.

She thought just knowing how they cooked the lobsters was terrible enough. Being forced to pick one out made the process a hundred times worse in her book.

She suspected they'd have to wait for a spot if it was a Saturday night in July instead of October. Although several customers enjoyed meals, only about half the restaurant's tables were occupied, so that wasn't the case tonight. And after leading the group past several booths and tables, the hostess paused at a table a few feet away from the double-sided, flagstone fireplace. Situated in the middle of the room, the wood fire burning inside it added both atmosphere and extra warmth. While the weather earlier had been mild for the time of year, the temperature had been dropping ever since the sun set.

The restaurant employee waited until they'd all sat before handing each of them a menu. Much like the sign out front, it featured the restaurant's name and a picture of a lobster. "Luke will be over shortly."

Maddie already knew what she wasn't having. However, the menu contained four pages and included everything from seafood to steak and salads, giving her plenty to pick from. "Does anyone have some recommendations?"

"I usually get either the cod piccata or the shrimp scampi." Instead of opening the dinner menu, Amari reached for the drink one the hostess had left. "Tonight, I'm getting the cod."

IF MADDIE HADN'T SUGGESTED they invite Colby and his fiancée to dinner, it wouldn't have occurred to Keith. He was glad she had, though, because he didn't know when he'd get another chance to spend time with Colby. But as much as he'd enjoyed hanging out with the couple and getting to know Amari, Keith was looking forward to getting back to their suite, where they could put the king-sized bed to good use again.

Last night, although they were all adults, he'd been unable to get past the fact his parents were sleeping on the other side of the wall. So even though he'd wanted to make up for the time they'd spent apart that week, he'd done nothing but kiss Maddie good night when they went up to his old bedroom.

When they returned from their walk earlier, he'd joined Maddie in the shower because waiting until later tonight had been beyond him. But, although he'd gone in planning to pleasure her until her legs gave out and she collapsed on the tiled bench, Maddie had other ideas. Eventually, though, they found their way to the bed. But, unfortunately, the wedding rehearsal made lingering impossible.

But that was behind them, and they had the rest of the night to enjoy each other, both in the bed and in the hot tub. He'd booked a presidential suite rather than any other type because those rooms contained a private hot tub, a feature none of the other suites at the resort had.

"Amari lived in the same dorm as you and Colby freshman year."

After pressing the button for the fourth floor, Keith watched the elevator doors close. "I don't remember her."

Maybe if they'd had some classes together, he would've remembered Amari, but roughly three hundred students called Browning Hall home his freshman year.

"They've also worked together for three years."

He'd caught pieces of Maddie and Amari's conversation while he and Colby talked football. So he knew Epic Gaming, the company Colby worked for, had come up.

"And you're telling me this why?" Amari seemed nice. However, at the moment, he had one thing on his mind, and it had nothing to do with Colby and his fiancée.

"You seemed worried when you found out he was marrying someone he'd only been with for a couple of months," she answered as the elevator reached their floor. "I figured it'd make you feel better if you knew they'd been friends longer than you and I have."

This afternoon he'd envisioned himself and Maddie in forty years asking someone to take a photo of them much the way the older couple had today, so he wasn't exactly in a position to criticize his friend's decision.

"I appreciate the intel. But right now, I don't want to talk or think about Colby and Amari."

Tossing her purse on the nightstand, Maddie turned toward him. "What do you want to do?"

Keith closed the distance between them and undid the top button of her blouse. "You in the bed." Brushing his lips against hers, he unfastened the following button. "In the hot tub." His fingers moved to the next button as he touched his mouth to hers again. "And in the shower."

"The chair could be fun." Maddie's fingers moved across his forearms toward his wrists, heating his skin and pushing his control to the brink. "I think the table is out, but the bench has promise." She nodded toward the upholstered bench at the foot of the bed as she grabbed both his wrists and pulled them away from her shirt.

"Where should we start?" She undid the last two buttons and slipped her arms out, letting the top land on the floor. Her eyes shifted toward the bed and then back to him as she slid the zipper on the side of her skirt down. Much like the top, her skirt landed forgotten on the floor. "We've already tested the bed. Should we use the hot tub next?"

Rather than answer, he feasted his eyes on the view before him. He'd thought it a little odd but hadn't questioned her when she went into the bathroom to get dressed. If anyone had asked, he would've said she was wearing a no-frills cotton bra and panties like she always did under the blouse and skirt when she walked out. And he would've never been more wrong in his life.

The black lace corset ended several inches above her waist, leaving her defined abs on display. A tiny triangle of black lace situated well below her navel completed the outfit—assuming it consisted of enough fabric to be classified as an outfit. Whatever the hell it was, Keith hoped she had more like it at home.

"Turn around." This outfit deserved to be viewed from all vantage points.

Maddie's right eyebrow inched up, and she crossed her arms as a hint of a smile pulled at her lips. "Excuse me?"

He'd play along tonight. "Please turn around."

"Well, since you said please."

The sight of her in the tiny thong almost brought him to his knees. "Are you trying to fucking kill me?"

She glanced over her shoulder at him. How she managed such an innocent expression, he had no idea. Yet, she did. "I have no idea what you're talking about."

Unable to resist, he ran his left hand over her ass while his right traveled down her stomach and under the lace covering her. "Tell me you have more like this at home." He kissed her neck as he slipped one finger inside her. Although he'd just touched her, she was already wet and ready for him.

He received a moan in response.

They'd have to test out the hot tub later. There was no way he could wait for it to fill with water. "What was that? I didn't hear you," he asked, undoing his belt with one hand.

Grabbing his wrist, she pulled his hand away and faced him again. "You'll have to wait and see," she said before taking care of the button and zipper on his pants. "You never answered me." She pushed his pants down, leaving him to free his ankles, and then turned her attention to the buttons on his polo shirt. "I think we should try the hot tub next. What about you?"

Keith yanked the shirt over his head and tossed it on the floor. "After."

"No." Placing her hands on his shoulders, she moved them down his body and slowly shook her head. "I don't want to." When her hands reached the waistband of his underwear, she paused. "But don't worry." Maddie kissed the pulse in his neck and then met his eyes. "I'll make sure you enjoy the wait while it fills with water," she said, running her hand down the length of him.

If she did that again, he'd come right there. "Start the water. I'll open the champagne."

TEN

"If I were any more relaxed, I wouldn't have a pulse," Maddie said.

Keith glanced in Maddie's direction in time to see her lick the chocolate off her bottom lip, drawing his attention to her mouth. Immediately, his mind brought up memories of how she'd used it and her tongue to pleasure him while they waited for the hot tub to fill up.

Until a second ago, he would've agreed with her. Now, thanks to the images going through his head and the fact he couldn't seem to get enough of Maddie, he was anything but relaxed.

Keith had slept with plenty of women, but he'd never desired anyone twenty-four seven or something damn close. He chalked it up to their relationship being new and the fact he'd fantasized about sex with Maddie for so long the first couple of weeks they were together.

That explanation no longer worked.

Not that it mattered, because he knew the reason.

Since college, whenever he dated a woman, it had always been about having fun and physical pleasure. Love had never played a role in his relationships.

Despite his past, Keith had gone into their relationship expecting more than just a good time and sexual gratification. Just how much more, he hadn't known.

Little signs pointing out that he loved her had been there for weeks. But he'd ignored them. What did he know about love? At least that kind. Yeah, he loved his family and would do anything for his friends, but that was different.

Today's run-in with the older couple had been like a sledgehammer driving the truth home.

He loved her. And assuming she didn't get sick of him, Keith wanted to spend the next fifty or sixty years with Maddie.

"I have a ton of vacation time. You must have a lot too. We should go on vacation when the holidays are over," Maddie said before finishing the wine in her glass and grabbing a grape off the plate.

While at the store, they'd bought not only cheese, crackers, and wine, but also fresh fruit and more chocolate. They'd been nibbling on all of it for the past twenty minutes.

She popped the fruit in her mouth and turned to look at him. "Someplace warm and on the ocean. Maybe Puerto Rico. Jasmine keeps telling me I'd love it there. If we can get off more than a week, maybe Hawaii. I don't want to be on a plane for that long and spend only a week there. Aruba might be nice too. I've been there twice, but it's been a while. What do you think?"

Her question didn't require any thought. Hell, if Keith thought they could both get a week or two off on such short notice, he would suggest they book something now and leave Monday morning. "Let's do it."

"Any preference on where we go?"

As long as it included a tropical location and some sandy beaches, the place didn't matter to him. "I don't care as long as you bring a few of those outfits you had on earlier, and we have a king-sized bed."

"Do you think about anything besides sex?"

Keith nodded. "Yeah, you. All the time."

"Is that so?" She didn't sound convinced.

He didn't share his feelings often. Tonight, he'd make an exception. "Who else would I think about?"

"Your friends? Maybe your family?"

"I don't love them." Leaning closer, he brushed his thumb across her shoulder and pressed a brief kiss against her lips. "I love you."

Maddie's eyes widened slightly, and Keith knew she hadn't expected to hear him say those three words tonight.

Keith hoped to hear something along the same lines from her. But instead, she asked, "You don't love your family?"

The woman could be impossible sometimes. "Maddie, you know what I mean."

Taking his hand, she entwined their fingers. "I love you too, but..." Maddie paused as if to torture him, because no one wanted the word "but" in the same sentence as "I love you too."

"You need to work on that. It's not healthy to focus on the same thing all the time, no matter what it is." She patted his cheek and grinned. "Maybe you should try to be more like me and find a hobby to occupy your thoughts. I'll even help you make a list."

"And what's your hobby?"

"Cooking."

Things like stamp collecting and knitting came to mind when he thought of hobbies. Cooking was something a person did because you had to eat.

"But we're talking about you, not me." Leaving the bed, she grabbed another bottle of wine from the mini fridge. "Besides having sex and eating chocolate, what do you enjoy doing?" she asked.

A guitar riff exploded from the clothes pile, letting him know he'd received a text message. The first one he'd gotten all day. He didn't expect it to be important, but he'd check the device anyway.

"I think playing the guitar would make an excellent hobby.

And you're good at it," she said while he extricated his pants from the pile.

As promised, Jen had found some videos of him playing in college and brought them with her to their parents' house on Friday night.

The sound repeated as he pulled the phone out of the pocket.

Since he hadn't received any more sexually explicit messages, he'd figured either the person realized they'd been sending them to the wrong Keith, as unlikely as that was, or they'd decided to stop.

Clearly, he'd been wrong.

Hi Keith. Do you miss me?

He didn't expect an answer, but he'd ask anyway.

Who is this?

You know who this is, sweetie.

Following the newest message, a video thumbnail popped up on the screen.

The intelligent thing would be to delete the entire thread, turn off the phone, and climb back into bed with Maddie. But, instead, his curiosity won out, and he pressed play.

Some 80s ballad he recognized from a movie assaulted his ears as a woman pleasuring herself filled the phone's screen. "Fuck."

When he hit play, he hoped to see whoever sent the message, but not this part of her.

"What's the matter?" Maddie asked.

Keith considered and dismissed making something up in the same breath. Then, handing her the phone, he drained the wine-glass she'd filled.

He heard the woman in the video moan.

"Who the hell sent you this?"

"I have no fucking idea." But he wished he did. Then maybe he could do something about it. What, he didn't know at the moment, but he'd figure something out.

Grabbing the wine bottle, Keith refilled his glass and took

another drink from it before telling Maddie everything. "Last week, I got a message from someone that read like a script to a porn movie. I told them they had the wrong person. The next day, I got another, and it included my name."

Maddie's mouth took on an unpleasant twist. And Keith couldn't tell if she was mad at him, the woman in the video, or both. His money was on the last.

"This woman doesn't have the wrong person." Maddie handed him back the phone and returned to the bed. "Why would a woman send you this kind of stuff now? And why isn't she sharing her name? What does she have to hide?"

I wish I knew.

"No clue."

"Do you remember going out with anyone who used a messaging app?"

He'd already asked himself that question and, not surprisingly, came up blank. It'd been about seven months since he stopped seeing Lisa, the woman he'd dated before Maddie. They'd been together for about two months. Before her, he'd gone out with Krystal a handful of times, but they'd never slept together. Between her and Molly, who he'd been with for about a month and a half, he'd gone to dinner with several women. But, as far as he remembered, none had used a messaging app.

"Nope."

"Anything in the video look familiar?"

Yeah, there was no missing the anger in Maddie's voice. Of course, he'd be ticked off if a guy sent Maddie anything similar, so he couldn't fault her. But he just hoped the anger was directed solely toward the wannabe porn star and not him, because he had done nothing to encourage whoever she was.

Keith shook his head. Only the lower half of the woman's body appeared in the video, and the little of the room visible didn't look familiar. "Believe me. I wish something did."

Hell, even a tattoo on the woman's thigh or hand might help him figure out who kept sending the messages. But either the mystery woman didn't have any or she had them somewhere not seen in the video.

"Have you thought about asking Lyle for help?"

There wasn't anything Lyle Cardi, just one genius in Elite Force's cyber division, couldn't do when it involved computers or smartphones. And he would've paid a visit to Lyle's desk already if this was work related. But it wasn't, and he didn't want Lyle to lose his job for using company resources for a personal matter. And Keith didn't want to lose his job either.

"Coleman would fire us both."

"Knowing Lyle, he has what he needs at home if it's possible to get this person's name." Maddie didn't sound as angry, but no one would ever classify her tone as cheerful either.

"Yeah, you're probably right."

Just wanted to remind you of what you're missing. Did you enjoy my present?

After reading the newest message, he handed the device to Maddie. He didn't need Maddie to believe he was hiding anything.

"I'll talk to Lyle on Monday." It didn't hurt to ask the guy. And if Lyle learned the mystery woman's identity, he'd figure out a plan for dealing with her then.

The familiar guitar riff came from the phone again, and Maddie gave the device back to him.

I'll be imagining it's you again tonight, Keith. I know you'll be thinking of me.

Before he received any more messages, Keith turned the device off.

AFTER PAYING THE DELIVERY GUY, Lisa closed the door and logged into the messaging app she liked to use on her iPad. It'd been days since she let Keith know she was thinking of him.

Hi Keith. Do you miss me?

How could he not? It'd been months since they'd been together.

Who is this? Keith's response appeared on the device before she even put the pizza box on the kitchen table.

If he asked that, maybe Maddie was close enough to read the messages, because he knew the text was from her. They were soul mates. Who else would it be?

After sending a reply, Lisa attached an edited version of the video she'd made for him last weekend.

While Lisa gave him time to watch, she grabbed one of the beers Shawn had brought over and settled into a chair. If she had to listen to her cousin and her stepbrother go at it for the next few hours, she was drinking his beer.

Just wanted to remind you of what you're missing. Did you enjoy my present?

He didn't answer, but it didn't matter. Lisa knew him. Keith had enjoyed the video, and he'd watch it again while thinking of her.

The sound of a headboard hitting the bedroom wall traveled down the hallway again.

Unfortunately, Shawn arrived after she'd changed into her pj's and finished almost an entire bottle of wine, making it unsafe for her to drive even if she felt like going out. Which, tonight, she didn't.

Shawn and Nicole had been going at it ever since.

Another thud, followed by her cousin's voice calling out Shawn's name, reached Lisa's ears. And Lisa's mind instantly brought up memories of being in Keith's bed. She'd had a lot of lovers, but none better than Keith. She never failed to orgasm with him. She couldn't say the same about some of the guys she'd screwed.

Since she couldn't be with him tonight, she'd again have to settle for pleasuring herself. Maybe she'd even make another video to send him.

I'll be imagining it is you again tonight, Keith. I know you'll be thinking of me.

After logging out of the messaging app, Lisa's thoughts turned to Maddie.

Like any good friend would do, she'd called Maddie on Thursday night to see how she was holding up. After the photos she'd sent her, Lisa had expected Maddie to say it was over between her and Keith. What woman wouldn't kick her boyfriend to the curb after receiving pictures of him with another woman?

Evidently, Maddie.

Instead of hearing that their relationship was over, Lisa had gotten a recap of Keith's explanation, which was the truth, and learned that things were fine between them.

Lisa made up her mind then and there. While her plan to come between Maddie and Keith might eventually work, she'd reached the end of her patience. The bitch stood in the way of her and Keith's happiness. Unfortunately for Maddie, that meant she needed to be removed permanently from his life. And although Lisa wasn't a violent person, she intended to make sure that happened.

Until the details were all worked out, Lisa figured maintaining their friendship was in her best interest. That was why, before ending their conversation, she'd asked Maddie if she'd go with her to see the new Anderson Brady movie this weekend. Even before she brought it up, Lisa had expected a no. The woman had spent most of the week in New York City. Doing precisely what, Lisa didn't know, although Maddie had mentioned it was for work. She'd want to spend the weekend with Keith, not her. And Lisa didn't blame her.

However, she hadn't anticipated learning that Maddie and Keith were heading to Maine for a wedding. And if any doubt had remained regarding what she needed to do, finding out they were going on vacation together erased it.

Even though she'd moved on to plan B, Lisa saw no reason

to stop sending Keith messages so he knew she was thinking of him. After all, everyone liked to know the person they loved was thinking of them when they weren't together. And since it'd been a few days since her last message and Maddie and Keith were together, tonight had seemed like the perfect time to send the little present she'd made last weekend. Unfortunately, she had no way of knowing if the bitch had been in the room when he watched. But Lisa hoped she had been.

She heard her cousin's bedroom door open and then close. Not long after, Shawn walked into the kitchen. He hadn't bothered to pull on a shirt, and a sheen of sweat covered his chest and stomach. Her stepbrother had an incredible body, and if he was half as good as Keith in bed, she couldn't fault Nicole for screwing Shawn whenever he called.

"Thanks for ordering the food. What did you end up getting?" Shawn asked, crossing the room to the refrigerator.

She'd only received a yes from Nicole and Shawn when she asked if they wanted her to add anything to her order for them. But Shawn ate almost anything, and she knew what her cousin usually ordered from Brando's Pizza.

"Pizzas and Brando's appetizer sampler. Did you get a new tattoo?"

She didn't think there was anything hotter than a guy with tattoos. Unfortunately, Keith only had one. At least, that was the case right now. Once they got back together, she'd convince him to get more. However, Shawn had eight or nine different tattoos on various parts of his body. Her favorite was the wolf on his left shoulder—or at least, it always had been. She liked the Celtic cross now on his upper back even more.

"Yeah, about a month ago."

Beer in hand, Shawn opened the takeout container on the table and pulled out a mozzarella stick. "I saw Jeremy at the gym this morning. He told me he saw you last night."

"Yeah, I stopped by his place. He's going to help me with a problem."

Her stepbrother didn't need a detailed explanation. Shawn was the one who'd introduced her to Jeremy the last time she needed help to get rid of a problem.

Nodding, Shawn lifted the beer toward his mouth. "He's good at that."

"Who are we talking about?" Nicole asked, joining them.

"Jeremy. I saw him last night. He's going to stop by either Tuesday or Wednesday."

Nicole held up her hand for a high five. "It's about time you moved on. Let me know when he's coming over, and I'll make sure I'm out."

Already planned to. "Will do."

She'd let Nicole believe what she wanted. Soon enough, her cousin would see that she was with Keith again.

Nicole checked inside both pizza boxes and then got a beer from the refrigerator. "Do you care which one we take with us?"

"I ordered the spinach and feta one for myself."

"I like the Hawaiian better anyway." Nicole snagged a chicken wing from the sampler and picked up the pizza box. "See you later."

She wasn't even through her second slice of pizza when the sound of Nicole moaning reached her again. Immediately her brain conjured up memories, and raw need spread through her body. Just like last night, she'd have to satisfy her body now. But soon, Keith would be the one doing it.

ELEVEN

Keith added his contribution to Spike's kitchen table. Earlier in the week, Spike had invited everyone over to watch tonight's football game. The last he'd heard, Neil, Salty, and Matt planned to come while everyone else on the team were maybes except for Maddie and Alex. They'd both turned down the invitation, claiming they'd rather watch paint dry than a football game.

"I thought I'd be the last one here." After leaving work, Keith stopped at Shooter's and grabbed his takeout order. Unfortunately, after his detour, he'd gotten stuck behind a three-car accident.

Although the game started in about twenty minutes, only Matt's car was in the driveway.

"Salty needed to stop by Kenzie's and let her dog out. Neil just said he was running late when he called. Christian let me know yesterday that he's not coming. His sister and her family made an unexpected stop in town, and he's spending the night with them. I haven't heard from anyone else," Spike answered. "But I don't expect to see Connor tonight. Becca's mom is visiting."

"I'd think that would make it more likely that Connor would be here instead of at home."

He'd never met Deanna Buchanan, Becca's mother, but he knew Connor was glad his girlfriend's mom lived five hours away in Connecticut.

Turning off the oven timer, Spike removed a casserole dish. Cheese and red peppers covered the top of whatever it was. "He's trying to get on his future mother-in-law's good side."

Connor and his girlfriend had been living together for months. So Keith, along with everyone on the team, suspected it was just a matter of time before he proposed. As far as Keith knew, Connor hadn't even bought a ring yet. But maybe he'd missed the announcement. He had been somewhat preoccupied lately.

"Did Becca take pity on Connor and say yes?" Unable to resist, Keith grabbed a buffalo wing from the container he'd brought. Although not as good as the ones Maddie made, the wings from Shooter's were excellent, and he'd spent the ride here smelling them.

Matt didn't waste any time adding a scoop of whatever Spike pulled from the oven to his plate, along with a handful of crackers. "Connor hasn't asked her yet. But he told me he's got the ring."

Spike left his front door unlocked when he expected company, and friends knew to let themselves in. Tonight, Neil entered the kitchen in time to catch only the last part of Matt's sentence. "Are we talking about Salty or Connor?"

It was a fair question, and one Keith would've asked if he'd walked in on the same conversation, because they all knew it was only a matter of time before both guys proposed.

"Connor," Spike answered. "Salty is waiting until the end of December. Kenzie has always wanted to see the ball drop on New Year's Eve in New York. So, he booked them a room within walking distance of Times Square that's costing him a small fortune. He's planning to ask her then."

Even in the middle of June, the cost of hotel rooms in New York City was ridiculous. He could only imagine the price tag on New Year's Eve.

"But Connor won't wait much longer," Spike said before opening the box Neil had brought and pulling out a beer bottle. "Experimenting again, or is this the same one you brought last time?"

Keith didn't get the appeal, because it seemed like far too much work for something you could buy on your way home, but Neil enjoyed brewing his own beer. And his coworkers benefited from his hobby.

"Something new. I played with the recipe for the porter Lyle brews. What he makes is good, but I like this one better."

Porters weren't his favorite type of beer, but he'd yet to dislike anything Neil brewed. Keith expected the same to be true of what he'd brought tonight.

"Hey, I forgot to ask. Was Lyle able to help you out?" Spike asked as he walked toward the living room.

When Keith had asked for his help, Lyle agreed without any hesitation. And since the employees in the cyber division rarely failed to get the information they were after, Keith expected to have a lead on the mystery woman. But, unfortunately, he was no closer to an answer now than before enlisting Lyle's help.

"He tried. But he couldn't get anything from the company. Something about her using a VPN when she set up her account, so her data is masked; you know how technical Lyle gets when he explains stuff. I only understood about half of what he said."

If Lyle was passionate about anything, it was technology. But unfortunately, he sometimes forgot that not everyone understood it as well as he did or cared how it worked as long as it did.

Matt added another slice of pizza to his plate before following Spike to the other room. "Who are you looking for?"

Outside of Spike, Maddie, and now Lyle, he had told no one about the little mystery he couldn't solve.

"Keith has a secret admirer," Spike said, switching off the

music and turning on the television. "She likes to send him erotic text messages."

He had received nothing since Tuesday night. This time, though, he deleted the attached video rather than hit play. However, it was only a matter of time before he heard from her again. "More like a stalker. And she's graduated to also sending me pornographic videos of herself."

Neil grinned. "How do I get a woman to do that?"

Keith would've made a similar joke if he was single. But tonight, he didn't find the comment amusing. "You'd have to pay them."

"Back to your mystery woman. She sent you videos, and you still don't know who she is?" Matt asked.

"Her face never appeared in the video. At least not the first one. I didn't watch the second she sent."

All amusement vanished from Neil's face, and he placed his hand over his heart. "Hey, I'll take one for you and watch it. If her face appears, I can let you know."

Neil was joking, but he made a good point. Maybe Keith shouldn't have deleted it without watching it. Just because he had seen no clues in the first one didn't mean there hadn't been some in the second.

"I deleted it as soon as I got it."

"Does Mad Dog know what's going on?" Spike asked, sitting in his usual spot. Keith had been to the guy's house to watch countless games and just hang out, and if they were inside, he sat nowhere but in the leather recliner. Keith suspected it had a permanent imprint of the guy's ass on it.

"Yeah. I had to tell Maddie last weekend. She was right next to me when I got the first video."

From the beginning, Spike had suggested Keith tell Maddie rather than have it come back to bite him in the ass. In hindsight, he should've listened. Thankfully, it had caused no problems between them. At least not yet. But if it continued, she might not be as forgiving.

"What did she say?" Matt asked around a mouthful of food.

Both Spike and Matt had worked with Maddie longer than him, so they knew her well. "Just what you'd expect her to."

"She's got to be someone you slept with," Matt said.

"No shit. Thanks, Captain Obvious. It never would've occurred to me that I know this woman."

Matt ignored Keith's insult and continued. "You didn't hear what I said, Wallace. She isn't someone you took to dinner once and then dropped her off at home. You had sex with her."

"Matt's right. You spent more than a couple of hours with her at a restaurant."

If his friends were right, it'd help narrow down the list of potential people, because while he'd taken out a lot of women, he hadn't slept with all of them. But plenty of names remained.

"Who was the woman that wanted to move in with you after like a month and a half?" Spike asked before stuffing a cracker loaded with the hot cheesy dip into his mouth.

"Lisa. But I don't think it's her. She was sweet but the stereotypical dumb blonde from the movies. She wouldn't know what a VPN is, never mind use one when she's on the internet."

"You said she was an actress," Spike said. "Maybe she wanted you to think she was a dumb blonde."

Lisa had probably told him every show and commercial she'd appeared in—she'd liked to talk about herself—but the only one he remembered was *Precinct 3*. And he only remembered that one because he'd enjoyed the police drama and had been disappointed when it got canceled after season one.

"Yeah, she's had a few minor roles in things and has done a couple of commercials. But she mostly records audiobooks." He'd never cared enough to ask what type of books or who wrote them. "But why would Lisa want me to think she's dumb?" He could understand pretending to be someone you weren't, but not acting like the main character from *Clueless,* a movie his sister Kristen had loved at one time.

"Who knows why women do anything they do?" Matt said,

lifting his beer bottle to his mouth. The oldest of five, Matt had four younger sisters. The oldest of the four had moved in with him a year ago after their parents insisted she get and keep a job for more than a month while she found her true calling.

"Don't let Mad Dog or Alex hear you say that." Neil grabbed his empty plate and stood.

None of them needed Neil to tell them that.

"I still don't think it's Lisa," Keith said.

And that was the problem. Everyone had their quirks, but no one from his past jumped out as a potential stalker. And even if Keith still had the phone numbers of every woman he'd spent more than five minutes with, which he didn't, he couldn't call them and ask if they'd been harassing him.

"Doesn't hurt to call her," Spike said.

"And what? Ask her if she's been sending me unwanted porn?"

"Whoever this woman is, she's unstable. When people like that start talking, sometimes they let things slip. You know that. If it is Lisa and you call her, she might ask if you enjoyed watching the videos."

He'd deleted Lisa's number from his contacts when he ended things with her. If he suspected it was her, getting it wouldn't be impossible. But unless he knew for sure, he didn't want to contact her. She'd called him every day for two weeks when he broke up with her back in the spring, either begging him to reconsider or telling him if he ever changed his mind to call her. He'd rather not have her think he was interested in getting back together and start calling him again on top of everything else he had going on.

WHENEVER HRT GOT TOGETHER, there was plenty of unhealthy but delicious food on hand. Tonight at Spike's house wouldn't be any different. And she would've accepted his invitation if, while enjoying the junk food, she didn't also have to hear Keith and the others swear at the television when a player didn't catch the football or a referee made a call they didn't like. Honestly, what was the point of yelling? The players and referees couldn't hear you, and even if they could, it wouldn't change anything.

So, while Keith was telling a referee he needed his eyesight checked, she'd be at Murphy's Tavern. However, it wasn't where she wanted to be. Since they'd returned from Maine, Keith had spent every night at her house. As much as Maddie enjoyed having him there, his presence meant she'd missed the last two episodes of her new favorite television series, a contemporary version of Jane Austen's classic *Emma*. Keith would enjoy it about as much as she did football. With Keith occupied, tonight would've been a perfect time to relax in some comfy pj's and watch the episodes while she waited for him.

But she'd said no so many times recently when Lisa asked her to go out, she'd felt bad about doing it again, which was why after Maddie showered, she'd be driving to the restaurant and parking her butt on a barstool instead of her comfortable sofa.

"Since you're single for the night too, do you want to grab dinner or something?" Alex asked as she opened her locker and pulled out her travel shower bag.

For convenience, she'd used the gym at work. Alex had walked in moments after Maddie hopped on the elliptical, and they'd finished their workouts at the same time.

"I'm meeting my friend Lisa at Murphy's. You're welcome to join us. I think you'd get along well with her." Alex got along with everyone.

"Maybe I will. I'm definitely not in the mood to go home tonight."

An hour later, when Maddie walked inside the pub and heard someone performing a well-known Whitney Houston hit, she wished she'd remembered that tonight was karaoke night. She'd never been brave enough to attempt karaoke, but she gave a lot of credit to those that did. It was one thing to sing while alone in the car. Hell, she did it all the time. Sometimes Maddie even sang along to a song while she cooked. However, it took either guts, a lot of alcohol, or true talent to stand up in front of strangers and belt out a song. And every Thursday night, customers, usually with either a lot of guts or alcohol in their bodies, grabbed the mic and stepped on the stage. However, the forty-something-year-old woman performing now while her friends in the audience cheered her on actually had some talent. Maybe the customers would luck out tonight, and a few more people who could sing would take the stage.

Maddie was almost at the bar when she spotted Lisa at one of the high pub tables. "I thought you'd be sitting at the bar," she said, pulling out the chair opposite Lisa and sitting down.

"This table opened up just as I walked in, so I grabbed it. I figured we'd be more comfortable here."

No doubt they would be. But the more comfortable they were, the longer Lisa might want to stay. If possible, Maddie wanted to be on her way home in under two hours so she could get in one episode before Keith got there.

"A friend of mine from work might join us. I didn't think you'd mind."

"No, of course not. The more the merrier," Lisa answered.

"So, are you ordering food or just drinks tonight?" Before her workout, she'd had a protein shake but had eaten nothing since lunch, so she was hungry. But if they stuck with only drinks, they wouldn't be there as long.

"Both. The author I'm working for expects the audio files tomorrow, so I spent the whole day listening for any errors in the studio. I haven't eaten since about nine o'clock this morning."

Oh well, so much for a quick cocktail and conversation. "What kind of book is it?"

She preferred to read rather than listen to audiobooks, but she could understand the appeal, especially for people who spent a lot of time commuting to work. However, she guessed some genres were better suited to audio than others.

"Women's fiction," Lisa answered, opening her menu. "I prefer to do either romances or horrors similar to Stephen King's *Salem's Lot*, but as long as the author is willing to pay my rate, I'll record just about anything."

Since Maddie was here, she might as well eat too. Rather than go straight for the menu, she reviewed the list of specials the server had left on the table. Everything on it sounded delicious, making it hard to decide on a meal.

"Romances and horrors seem about as different as you can get."

"And that's why I love those types of projects. So much from other genres overlaps, but I've yet to record a true horror with any romance in it."

Maddie had never read a book that incorporated the two, but that didn't mean it didn't exist. A reader could find almost anything if they looked hard enough. "What's your least favorite genre, then?"

"Probably science fiction and fantasy," Lisa said, lifting her water glass to her mouth. "When authors ask me to narrate a book similar to *Star Trek* or *Firefly,* I cringe.*"*

"Not a *Star Trek* fan?"

She'd known of *Star Trek*. Who on planet Earth didn't? But before Keith, she'd never watched a single episode or movie. Unlike the *Star Wars* ones, which she'd seen many thanks to Spencer, who'd watched them repeatedly as a kid. Even now, he'd occasionally park his ass on the sofa and spend a Sunday watching all of them.

Keith had been appalled when he found out how little she knew about *Star Trek*. And over the past two months, they'd been working their way through the episodes in the original series. When they finished with those, Keith insisted they needed to watch the first six movies, which included the original cast. After that, he planned to move on to the *Star Trek: The Next*

Generation series. While Maddie didn't expect to ever be as big a fan as him, she'd enjoyed what she'd watched so far.

"Hell no. But my previous boyfriend was a huge science fiction fan. He even watched those terrible shows from the sixties and seventies. I don't know what was worse about them, the costumes or the lousy special effects."

She couldn't argue with Lisa there. The special effects were awful, and some of the costumes left her scratching her head.

"Sounds like he'd get along well with Keith. He's got a model replica of the *Defiant* that his sister bought him. He's even attended a couple of Star Trek Conventions."

Even non-fans knew the *Enterprise* was *the* ship in the *Star Trek* world. So she'd initially assumed the model was some version of it. Keith quickly corrected her and explained that the *Defiant* was from *Deep Space Nine*, his favorite series in the Star Trek universe.

Lisa made a face and shook her head. "I'd rather sit through a lecture on how to do my taxes than go to one of those conventions."

A year ago, Maddie would've said something similar. "It might not be too bad." Spotting Alex near the bar, Maddie waved to get her attention.

"I'll let you go to one, and then you can tell me about it," Lisa said.

Alex joined them, a glass of wine already in hand. "I forgot Thursday night is karaoke night."

"Yeah, me too," Maddie said before making introductions.

Their waiter arrived at the table a moment later, putting any conversation on hold.

TWELVE

Lisa had it all planned out. First, Maddie would meet her at Murphy's, a place she'd picked because she knew none of the security cameras in the building or the parking lot worked. According to her friend Danny, the restaurant's assistant manager, they hadn't worked in over a year, and the owner had no intentions of fixing or replacing the system.

During dinner, the pill in her purse would find its way into Maddie's drink. Lisa didn't know what it was. However, Jeremy assured her it would make Maddie drowsy and appear drunk, so no one would find it odd when Lisa helped her outside and to her car. And since the cameras didn't work, there would be no record of them being together.

Then she'd drive to the abandoned warehouse on Fowler Street and meet Jeremy, who would do the actual dirty work. Lisa didn't need a man to take care of things for her, but why get your hands dirty if you didn't need to? Especially when Jeremy took such enjoyment in his work, and since he was helping her, it was the least she could do.

She had to put everything on hold now because Maddie had invited a damn friend to join them. It had taken all her self-control not to react when Maddie told her. She'd been waiting over a week to see Maddie. Before today, every time she'd asked, Maddie had plans. And after tonight, who knew how long it might be before Lisa saw her again?

"You look familiar, but I don't know from where," Alex said, after placing her dinner order.

Oh, I know where.

Not long after Lisa and Keith began dating, they'd been walking into Murphy's one night as Alex and a man exited. Both couples stopped long enough to say hello. Lisa didn't remember if they had even made any introductions. And tonight, when Maddie's friend sat at the table, she'd never been happier that she'd cut and dyed her hair in August.

"I've done some television commercials, and I had a small role on *Precinct 3*."

If Alex assumed that was why Lisa looked familiar, she wouldn't spend more time thinking about it. The last thing she needed was for Alex to recall their brief encounter and mention Lisa's connection to Keith.

Alex nodded as she lifted her wineglass. "Yeah, that must be it. I enjoyed that show. I was bummed when they canceled it."

"You and me both."

Lisa had thought her career would finally take off when she got the role. Then, just like that, she was back to recording audiobooks while auditioning for any part she could get. To date, she'd only landed a few more television commercial jobs.

"So, how much yelling do you think is going on over at Spike's house?" Alex asked.

Thank you.

If Alex was wondering about what was happening at someone else's house, the woman had accepted Lisa's reason for why she looked familiar and dismissed the thought from her mind.

"Keith and a few other guys we work with are watching the football game tonight," Maddie explained before answering

Alex. "It'll depend on the teams playing. Keith probably told me, but I don't remember."

"So, you two work together?" Lisa asked.

"That's how we met," Maddie answered before turning her attention to Alex. "You started at the firm, what, two months after me?"

"Something like that."

"And is Spike the hot guy I saw you and Keith in here with that has a girlfriend?" Lisa didn't care who Spike was, but it seemed like an appropriate question.

Maddie shook her head as the waiter set down their drinks. "No, that was Connor you saw with us. Spike's single."

"And frigging gorgeous. I'm talking panty-melting, drool-worthy gorgeous," Alex added. "The man should be in Hollywood making movies or something. I almost wish he was my type."

"What makes him not your type?" Lisa asked.

"Family is important to Spike. He once told me he wanted to have three or four kids. I'm not interested in that. The only diapers I ever plan to change is if I have any nieces or nephews."

Lisa wasn't for or against having children. She'd simply never thought about it. Now that Alex mentioned them, though, she wondered what Keith's take on the subject was. When they were together, he'd never mentioned children except to say he had a niece who lived in Rhode Island.

"You sound like my brother," Maddie replied. "It's too late now, but maybe I should've set you and Spencer up."

"Even if things don't work out with Brandon, I'll pass. Spencer is a nice guy, and I like him. But I made the mistake of dating a friend's brother in college and will never do it again."

"Does Brandon work with the two of you too?" Of course, who they worked with was irrelevant, but asking allowed Lisa to control the conversation.

"No, we're both regulars at a café near my house. And one Sunday morning, we just started talking. That was about two months ago, I think. Last night, he invited me to his mom and stepdad's house for Thanksgiving. So we're going there for dinner, and then after, we'll head to my parents' house for dessert so that he can meet my family."

Maddie handed out the small appetizer plates the waiter had left when he delivered their drinks. "Sounds like things are going well."

"We're not planning any romantic getaways like you and Keith, but yeah, so far, things are great," Alex answered as the waiter set down the appetizer sampler they'd ordered in addition to entrees.

Lisa's hand froze before it reached her drink. "You and Keith just went on vacation."

"We were only gone for three nights, and one of them we spent at his parents' house, so I'm not sure it qualifies as a vacation. So, we're planning a trip to Puerto Rico in December."

"I forgot about your long weekend in Maine. Did you guys have fun?" Alex asked as she added food to her plate.

Lisa could've slapped Alex for asking that question because she didn't want to hear anything about Maddie and Keith's weekend away.

"We did. I got to meet Keith's family before we drove up to Maine. And Keith went all out and booked us a hotel suite with a fireplace and hot tub."

Lisa stabbed the stuffed mushroom on her plate and wished it was Maddie's heart instead as the bitch shared the details from her time in Maine.

"He even arranged for there to be flowers, chocolates, and champagne in the room when we checked in."

"Keith, as in the Keith Wallace we work with, did that?" Alex asked. "Are you sure he wasn't a lookalike?"

Laughing, Maddie nodded and added a smothered potato skin to her plate. "Surprised the hell out of me too. But it's not the first time he's bought me flowers. Keith can be romantic when he wants to be."

He'd never bought her flowers or booked them a hotel suite. Hell, he'd never even taken her on vacation or introduced her to his family.

"Since you had a private hot tub in the room, is it safe to assume you guys put it to good use?" Alex asked.

"Yep, as well as the large shower stall and the king-sized bed."

Pain shot up her wrist as her fingernails dug into her palm, and Lisa forced her hand to relax. This night was rapidly going from bad to worse.

"I've never been to Maine, but I know Brandon's aunt and his younger brother live there. Where did you guys stay? Maybe if we ever go up to visit and it's close to his family, we can go there."

"We were at the Admiral's Resort in Ogunquit. I'd have to ask Keith for the address. But it was very nice. I think you'd like it there."

"Brandon's brother is in Portland, and I think he said his aunt lives in Old Orchard Beach. Do you know if either is close to where you stayed?"

"No idea. Ask Keith; he might know." Maddie shrugged and pulled her beeping phone from her purse. "Keith said Spike's house lost power," she said after reading the text message. "If it's not back on soon, he's heading to my house."

Keith shouldn't be going to Maddie's house. After leaving his friends, Keith should either be coming to see her or heading to his apartment and waiting for her. He knew that. Keith was only trying to make her jealous, as usual. And damn, it was working.

"Does he know you're out?" Lisa asked.

Maddie finished typing a message and put her phone on the table. "Yes, but Keith has a key, so he can let himself in. I don't have to worry about rushing home."

If Maddie had given Keith a key to her house, did that mean she had one for Keith's apartment?

Lisa had one. She'd found it in the junk drawer in his kitchen a few weeks before he ended their involvement. Considering all the crap Keith kept in there, he'd probably never noticed it was gone. And if he had gone looking for it, he most likely assumed he'd misplaced the thing.

And not only did Lisa have a key, but she'd used it more than once. Sitting in his kitchen or lying on his bed helped her feel closer to him.

The first time she'd let herself in had been about a month after they had broken up. She'd driven to his apartment complex, curious about what he was up to. When she saw his motorcycle wasn't in the parking lot, she took a chance and went inside. Her next visit came after Maddie mentioned Keith was traveling for work and wouldn't be home for a couple of days. Her most recent visit had been last weekend while Maddie and Keith were in Maine. Since she knew he wouldn't be home until Monday, she'd spent all day Saturday there.

"Does anyone want the last stuffed mushroom?" Alex asked.

She'd lost much of her appetite when Maddie started talking about her and Keith's time away. "I'm all set."

"It's all yours." Maddie gestured toward the plate as she picked up her cell phone again.

Alex added the mushroom and a chicken wing to her plate. "Since we're on the topic of Keith, did you decide if you're going to ask him to move in with you?"

Lisa choked on the wine she'd swallowed, and both women looked at her as she coughed.

"Are you okay?" Maddie asked, genuine concern in her voice.

No.

"It went—" She coughed again. "—down the wrong way."

Maddie waited until Lisa stopped coughing before answering Alex's question. "Yeah, I'm going to ask him. He spends more time at my house than at his place, so it makes little sense for him to keep paying rent. I don't know when his lease agreement is up, though, so he might want to wait."

"You haven't been together even six months. Are you sure that's a good idea?" Pulling out her cell phone, Lisa sent a brief message to Jeremy, so he knew the plans for tonight had changed.

"We've known each other for almost two years. I'm sure about it."

Pure hatred washed through her body. The roomful of customers was the only thing preventing Lisa from plunging the steak knife on the table into Maddie's chest.

Rather than befriending her and trying to come between Maddie and Keith, Lisa should've gotten rid of the woman the day she followed Maddie home from Keith's apartment building. If Lisa had done that, she would've been the one Keith took to Maine. Right now, he would be on his way to her house after the game and would spend the night in her bed. And instead of Maddie and Keith planning a romantic trip for next month, they would be.

It was time to correct her mistake because Maddie had to go. And if it couldn't happen tonight, it would happen in the next day or two.

THIRTEEN

A PICTURE FEATURING ONE OF THE RESORT'S MANY POOLS greeted Maddie when she flipped to the next page in the folder. Unlike the other three pools, though, this one contained a swim-up bar. She'd stayed at a lot of places and swam in a lot of hotel pools, but she'd never used one with a swim-up bar. And she was looking forward to trying it out next month. But, of course, it wasn't the only resort amenity she was looking forward to enjoying.

When she'd called the Great Getaways Travel Agency and described the type of vacation they wanted, their price range, and what amenities they'd like at their hotel, Ava came back with three possible resorts. They'd dismissed one immediately because, while the cheapest, it was the furthest from the beaches, and the only amenity from their list appeared to be a small outdoor pool. Maddie and Keith had agreed that while they didn't need the resort to have an Olympic-size pool, it needed one large enough to fit more than five people at a time.

The other two options had been comparable in every way except one. The Sherbrooke Caribe Beach Resort had its own beach, which only hotel guests could access, while the other had lovely views of the ocean, but guests needed to drive and use a public beach. So, although slightly more expensive, they'd opted for the Sherbrooke resort. And tonight, on her way home, she'd stopped at the travel agency to pay the balance on the trip and pick up the final paperwork. Since she was doing that, Keith offered to grab takeout after he finished his workout. And she expected him any minute. About forty minutes ago, he'd let her know he was leaving the gym and going to Asahi, a restaurant that prepared both Japanese and Chinese cuisine.

Maddie's eyes scanned the list of water activities guests could engage in at the resort. Scuba diving and paddle boarding, she recognized. In fact, she enjoyed paddle boarding and often went when she visited her parents, since they lived close to the beach. Sea trekking and snuba, she'd never heard of, but she was open to trying almost anything. One thing she did plan to do at least once was rent an inflatable tube and just float on the ocean while she worked on her tan. Already her summer tan had faded, and the winter hadn't even started yet.

Curious about both activities and with nothing better to do, she typed "sea trekking" into the search engine on her phone.

"You can barely see two feet in front of you tonight." Keith's voice carried into the kitchen, pulling her attention away from her search results. "I didn't even know it was supposed to rain today."

"The forecast called for it, but not until much later. Looks like they got it wrong again."

Keith stopped at the table long enough to set down the takeout bag and kiss her cheek before crossing to the cupboard for plates. "Is that the info on our trip?"

"Yeah. I was just looking over the activities the resort offers. Hey, do you know what snuba is?"

"Never heard of it. Why?" Rather than return to the table, he opened the fridge. "Do you want anything to drink?"

"Whatever you're having is good." Maddie looked back at her phone and the search engine results for sea trekking. "It's listed as something we can do at the resort, along with sea trekking, scuba diving, and paddle boarding."

"No idea of what sea trekking is either."

"According to the internet, sea trekking is a guided underwater walking tour to depths between three meters to nine meters depending on the location." Maddie did some rough calculations in her head. "Which is roughly nine to thirty-two feet. This web page says it's suitable for anyone over eight years old and doesn't require previous diving experience."

Maddie liked the sound of that. She'd considered learning to scuba dive a few times. Once, she even found a place nearby that offered the certification course. But, in the end, she'd decided against it. While she loved the idea of seeing life under the ocean, the realization of all that could go wrong while at such depths stopped her.

Keith handed her a can of ginger ale and took the seat next to her. She'd started keeping soda in the house, more for him than herself. But occasionally, Maddie did like some ginger ale or root beer. Cola or anything with the word "diet" before it, though, she passed on all the time.

"It could be interesting to try. What's it say about snuba?" Keith asked.

"Just about to look it up." Maddie typed the unfamiliar term and waited for the internet to do its magic.

Opening one container, Keith picked a spicy salmon roll from it and popped it into his mouth before removing the covers from the others. "Do you want to eat in here or in the living room while we watch TV?"

Monday morning, Keith and Spike were escorting Stan Bond on another of his Venezuelan trips. When Ax had informed them, her initial reaction had been "better them than me." Disappointment had followed because the assignment meant Keith would be gone for five days. And since he was leaving soon, they'd opted to stay home and watch television rather than go out with friends. Keith wanted to finish the third and final season of the original *Star Trek* series this weekend so they could move on to the movies when he got back. Honestly, she didn't care either way.

Opting for a tuna roll, she clicked on the top result from her newest internet search. "Other room. We'll be more comfortable. And to answer your other question, snuba is a cross between snorkeling and scuba."

"I've done both and prefer scuba." Keith added several pieces of sashimi, some she couldn't identify, and a few sushi rolls to his plate. "But hey, if you want, we can try every activity the hotel offers," he said, filling the space left with the restaurant's house fried rice.

She'd had fried rice from many places, but Asahi made the best, in her opinion. She could happily eat it as a meal.

"But I won't object if you want to lounge naked on our balcony all week drinking cocktails, either. You booked us a room with a balcony, right?"

"It has a balcony as well as a king-sized bed. But no in-room hot tub. If we want to use one, we'll have to go to the pool area. There's two down there."

"Won't be nearly as much fun."

She agreed with him. At the same time, though, she liked the idea of sitting in a hot tub while sipping a tropical drink and watching the ocean. "In that case, what do you think about getting a couple's massage one day?"

The resort had a full-service spa that offered everything from facials and pedicures to massages.

"Is it something you want to do?" Keith asked, leaving the kitchen.

Plate and drink in hand, Maddie followed him. "They sound relaxing, and the spa has a few different packages."

"Then let's do it."

"The resort recommends you book well in advance to guarantee you get an appointment. This weekend, we should look over the packages and schedule one."

"Just pick whichever one you want. I trust your judgment."

In that case, Maddie already knew which one she'd book for them. "I'll call and make a reservation tomorrow. What time do you need to be at Salty's in the morning?"

Keith scrolled through the old *Star Trek* episodes until he reached the one labeled "Day of The Dove." "Everyone's getting there around ten o'clock. I don't know why I agreed to help him."

"He probably offered you free beer and pizza."

Keith threw her a dirty look and tossed the remote on the table. "You're hilarious. Hopefully, the rain won't stop, and Salty will want to wait to move his stuff."

"Sorry, the forecast for tomorrow is cool but sunny, my friend. Besides, if it rains, you'll just have to help him some other time."

"Maybe he'd change his mind and hire a moving company."

She'd known it was only a matter of time before Salty and his girlfriend, Kenzie, moved in together. The unknown had been which house they'd live in. The two homes were nearly identical and on the same street. "He's moving next door. I wouldn't want to waste the money on movers either."

"He's still going to owe me one. I don't care how much beer and pizza there is to eat tomorrow."

Maddie had intended to bring up Keith moving in with her when she got home last night. However, she'd left Murphy's later than she'd planned and found Keith asleep on the sofa when she got home. He'd woken up long enough to get into bed, but he'd been out again as soon as his head hit the pillow. And this morning, he'd been up and out the door before she woke up. So now seemed like as good a time as any to bring up the topic.

Grabbing the remote, she paused the television. She didn't want to hear Captain Kirk tell the crew to go to red alert while discussing where Keith would call home.

"I've been thinking about this all week. You spend most of

your time here. I don't think you've slept in your apartment in over a week."

"It's been longer than that. The last time I slept there was when you were in New York City with Lady Haverston and her granddaughter."

Yeah, he was right. "So basically, you're paying rent for a place to keep your stuff. I don't know how much longer you've got on your lease, but I think you should move in with me."

"It's up for renewal at the end of January. I got an email reminding me this week, but I have signed nothing yet."

Talk about good timing.

"Sounds like you've got time, so you don't need to give me an answer now if you want to think about it."

"What's there to think about? I've been hoping you'd ask, because it didn't make sense for me to ask you to move into my apartment. I'll let management know I'm not renewing my lease next week when I get back from babysitting Bond."

THE METEOROLOGIST HAD BEEN wrong about yesterday's weather, but not today's. When Keith opened the blinds on the kitchen door, a blue sky and puffy white clouds greeted him. And once again, he mentally kicked himself for agreeing to help Salty move. Although, on the positive side, since Keith was helping Salty, the guy wouldn't be able to say no when Keith asked for help moving the stuff from his apartment to Maddie's house. Or at least some of his things. Not everything he owned would fit here. Some things he didn't care about. A few items, like the kitchen table, he'd barely used, and he'd find somewhere to donate them. Other objects, though, he'd have to either put in a storage unit or ask Maddie to make room for them. He knew Salty had a similar issue. And that was why today they were moving some of Salty's belongings over to Kenzie's house and some to a storage unit.

Keith removed the mug from under the coffee maker and put it on the counter as Maddie walked into the kitchen. "This one is for you."

"I knew I kept you around for a reason." Brushing her lips against his, Maddie reached for the mug.

"You can do better than that." He grabbed her hand before it reached the coffee mug.

"Probably, but do you deserve better?"

"I did make you some coffee." Keith slid his fingertips up her arms and to her bare shoulders.

"True. But I'm making dinner tonight for us, so I think that makes us even." Maddie stepped closer and put her arms around his waist. "Now that I think about it, you're going to owe me. Dinner will require a lot more than hitting brew on a machine."

He wished she hadn't bothered pulling on her tank top as his hands slipped from her shoulders and covered her breasts. Despite the material covering them, her nipples hardened against his palms, and he imagined closing his lips around one as he teased the other.

"Bad idea." Maddie pulled his hands away and moved them back to her shoulders.

"I don't know what you're talking about." She knew him well.

Maddie made a sound somewhere between a laugh and a snort. "Bull. Your dick is doing the thinking again, and we both know it. But if you want breakfast before you leave, it will have to wait because it's getting late."

He didn't have to like it, but she was right. Even if Salty ordered pizzas later, he needed something to eat before he headed out this morning. Before his hands found their way south again, Keith dropped his arms by his side and stepped away.

Although he didn't prepare complicated meals, he could handle the basics. "I'm going to make eggs. Do you want some?"

"Nah, I'm going to have a bagel with peanut butter."

A bagel with peanut butter was more a snack to hold you over between meals than breakfast in his book. "Can you pop one in the toaster for me too?" He'd need something to go with his eggs and bacon.

Nodding, Maddie sipped her coffee before grabbing the bagels from the breadbox.

"What are your plans for today?" Keith asked, cracking three eggs into a bowl and beating them.

Maddie shrugged and sliced an everything bagel in half. "Getting the stuff to make dinner and reading my new book."

"Why don't you come with me instead?" The more people helping with the move, the faster they'd get it done.

"Salty didn't ask me to help."

It was one of the lamest excuses he had heard in a long time. After pouring the eggs into a pan, he grabbed the bacon. He preferred breakfast sausage with his eggs, but he'd eat what Maddie had on hand.

"He would've asked you too if you'd been there when he brought it up. And you know it."

"Maybe. Maybe not. But I don't want to ruin guy time with your friends." She patted his cheek before getting out the peanut butter. "Don't worry about me; I'll survive while you're off having fun."

She made it sound like they were going to Shooter's and playing pool.

"What time do you think you'll be home, so I know when to have dinner ready?"

Home. He liked the sound of that. Even before Maddie gave him a key, Keith felt as if he was home whenever there.

Unlike his apartment, Maddie's house was more than a place where she kept her clothes and slept. Her personality filled the rooms, and although it looked nothing like his parents' house, Maddie's place gave off the same vibe. Not that he'd ever tell the guys he worked with that because they'd laugh their asses off. However, as much as Keith loved it here, Maddie was the real reason he always felt he was home. And he'd been hoping for weeks she'd ask him to move in. He'd even held off signing a new lease agreement, whereas last year, he would've done it right after getting the reminder email.

"Beats me. If it helps, I can let you know when we're heading over to the storage facility to unload the truck."

"I thought you guys were just moving everything to Kenzie's?"

I wish.

"Kenzie can't fit all of Salty's furniture, so they're both putting some stuff in a storage unit."

Maddie spread a thick layer of peanut butter over each half of the toasted bagel and then covered it with an equally thick layer of Nutella. "I didn't think of it, but that makes sense. They can't fit two houses' worth of furniture into one."

Rather than add the knives to the sink, Maddie removed the remaining peanut butter from one with her finger and then licked it off. Although an innocent action, it immediately brought to mind where her tongue had been last night, and it had Keith reconsidering how badly he needed breakfast before he left.

"I have an empty bedroom, but there's still not going to be enough room for everything in your apartment, so we'll have to do the same thing."

The smell of bacon filled the kitchen, and his stomach sent a message to his brain, demanding food and putting his body's other wants on hold. "I was thinking about that while I made coffee. When I'm over at the storage place, I'll see about renting a unit."

About an hour later, Keith walked outside and wished his motorcycle was parked in the driveway. While there was no law against using it when snow covered the ground and the temperatures plummeted to below zero, Keith never did. With winter closing in on them, today might be the last opportunity he got to use it. Unfortunately, it remained in the parking lot at his apartment complex. If his place were on the way to Salty's, it would make sense to stop and switch vehicles, but his apartment was in the opposite direction. If the weather was similar tomorrow, he'd see if Maddie wanted to go for one last ride before he put it to bed for the winter.

By the time Keith pulled up behind Spike's car, a rented U-Haul occupied Salty's driveway, and his front door was open. And as he pulled the keys from the ignition, Connor parked behind him.

"Remind me again why we agreed to help with this?" Connor asked as they crossed the lawn toward the house.

"Because you're both good friends," Kenzie answered as she headed down the walkway carrying a cardboard box with the word "bedroom" written on the side. And rather than head for the truck or her house, she stopped alongside them.

He knew the box Kenzie held was just one of many waiting for them inside. "I think it's more like because we're idiots."

"Well, we already know that about you, but that doesn't explain what I'm doing here," Connor said.

Kenzie sighed. "Fine, then you're here, Connor, because Ryan helped when you moved into Becca's house." Kenzie's voice reminded him of his sister's when Kristen was frustrated and dealing with her daughter. "If you guys need anything to drink or get hungry, snacks are on my kitchen table. Help yourself. I left a cooler full of drinks in there too. And later on, I'm going to order pizzas from Uncle Tony's."

Later, he'd take Kenzie up on the offer. But, right now, he'd get to work because the sooner they started, the sooner he'd be back at Maddie's.

"Mad Dog not helping us today?" Connor asked as they entered Salty's house.

"I tried to get her to come. She refused."

"She might have terrible taste in men, but she's smarter than us."

"I always thought the same thing about Becca. It's funny

how similar they are." His favorite guitar riff followed Keith's comment.

"I'm going to say it's a love note from either Mad Dog or your secret admirer."

Connor had known Maddie longer than Keith. "Do you see Maddie sending me love messages?"

"Hey, I never saw Mad Dog wasting her time with you either, but she's been doing that for how many months now?"

He doubted the message was from Maddie, since he'd just left her. As he pulled the device from his back pocket, Keith hoped to find a message from one of his sisters. Hell, he'd even prefer another one of those political surveys he'd been getting to a text from his unknown stalker.

A phone number he didn't recognize greeted him rather than the username Keith had come to dread.

We'll be together soon. I promise.

Yep, not the political survey he'd hoped. But maybe this message would be helpful. Assuming the woman was using her phone and not someone else's or a cheap prepaid one, Lyle should be able to get a name by using the number. And if Lyle tracked the number back to a prepaid phone instead, he'd at least be able to get a location for it. That would help him determine who this person was. Once he knew that, he could finally deal with her.

After shooting off a brief message to Lyle, Keith stuck the phone back in his pocket and entered Salty's house.

"All right, Salty, where are we starting today?" Keith asked.

FOURTEEN

Lisa turned onto Hearth Stone Road. Since Thursday night, she'd thought only about one thing: being alone with Maddie and finally eliminating her from Keith's life. She'd hoped to do it yesterday. But unfortunately, when she drove by around seven o'clock, Keith's truck was parked in the driveway, forcing her to abandon her plan again.

Fingers crossed, things would go her way today.

After coming around the slight bend in the road, Maddie's house came into view. Lisa smiled as joy bubbled up in her chest because neither Keith's truck nor his motorcycle was anywhere in sight.

Her first instinct was to pull into the empty driveway and ring the bell. However, her common sense kicked in before she made a colossal mistake and did it. The absence of a vehicle didn't mean Keith wasn't there. It also didn't mean Maddie didn't have a guest. The damn woman seemed to have an endless list of male and female friends. Lisa needed to verify that one, Maddie was home, and two, she was alone before making a move.

It took effort, but she maintained a constant speed down the road. At the stop sign, she turned left, exiting Maddie's neighborhood, and drove to the nearby shopping plaza on Bridge Street. As usual, numerous cars filled the lot, and Lisa opted for a spot away from the complex and the other vehicles.

Before pulling out her cell phone, Lisa closed her eyes and crossed her fingers.

Please be at home and alone.

Hey, are you busy?

Lisa held her breath as she waited for a response to the text message.

Maddie didn't keep her waiting long.

I'm grocery shopping. Why? What's up?

Although not the response Lisa wanted, it was better than some alternatives.

I need to talk to someone. Can I come over when you get home if Keith's not there?

It took longer for Maddie to answer her second message, and Lisa feared she would either say she wasn't going home once she finished shopping or that Keith was meeting her at the house. Either answer would force her to abandon her plan again. And she was running out of time. Thursday night, Maddie never specified when she planned to ask Keith to move in. For all Lisa knew, Keith had already agreed and was at his apartment packing up his belongings right now.

Keith's helping a friend. I should be home in about 30 minutes. Meet me then.

Euphoria flowed through her. Soon, no one would stand between her and Keith.

With her goal almost within her grasp, she didn't want to make any mistakes now. And since Maddie had never invited her over, Lisa shouldn't know where the bitch lived.

What's your address?

10 Hearth Stone Rd. It's a gray house with blue shutters.

Instead of typing another message, Lisa responded with a thumbs-up emoji.

SINCE KEITH WOULDN'T BE BACK for a few hours, Maddie had been looking forward to experimenting with the new recipe she'd found on her go-to cooking website and doing a little reading. She'd purchased her favorite historical romance author's latest book Tuesday when it was released, but she hadn't started it.

But when a friend said they needed to talk, a person couldn't say no. Well, some people could, but she'd never been able to. So while a visitor ruled out diving into her newest book, she could listen and cook at the same time. And she might need to do that.

According to the recipe, the steak tips needed to marinate for at least two hours in the refrigerator. Then, before she cooked them, they needed to sit out at room temperature for thirty minutes. The prep for the twice-baked potatoes, a recipe she'd come up with herself, took her about twenty minutes, and then they required about fifty minutes in the oven. She'd like Lisa to be gone and dinner ready for around when Keith got back. But if she could only have one of the two, it'd be the first because, in her experience, the old saying about three being a crowd was usually true.

Since the marinade was the key to everything, she prepared it as soon as she returned home. And about forty-five minutes after Lisa's text, she was about to pour it over the steak tips when the doorbell rang.

Until now, the only time she'd seen Lisa without makeup had been at the gym. But it wasn't the only thing that seemed off about her when Maddie opened the door. Something about her eyes wasn't quite right, but she couldn't put her finger on it. Maybe the reason Lisa needed to talk had something to do with whatever wasn't right.

"Come on in."

"Thanks for letting me come over."

"Anytime."

"How long have you lived here?" Lisa asked, following Maddie into the kitchen. "When I was looking for a house, I looked at one in this neighborhood."

Maddie had to think before she answered. In some ways, it felt like she'd lived there forever, and in others, it seemed like she'd moved in last month. "Almost three years."

It seemed hard to believe, but she'd purchased the home not long after she started working for Elite Force Security.

"Do you want something to drink?" She might not want Lisa to stay long, but a good hostess at least offered their guest a beverage.

"Some wine would be great. I don't care what kind. But if you don't have any, whatever you're having is fine."

Not only had she been thinking more like tea or coffee when she asked, but the wine she'd bought was for dinner tonight. Since the bottles were nowhere in sight, Lisa would never know she had some. "I forgot to pick some up while I was out, so I don't have any wine. I was going to have some coffee. Or I can make you tea."

"Coffee is fine."

Lisa opted for the chair Maddie generally used at the table and hung her oversized purse on the back of it. The thing was large enough to hold a bowling ball, and Maddie couldn't even imagine carrying around so much stuff to need such a large purse.

She had too many friends to remember how they all preferred their coffee. "Do you like cream and sugar in your coffee?"

"Yep. But I'll use milk if you don't have cream."

While the coffee machine brewed the first cup, Maddie mixed the steak tips and the marinade together.

"Are you celebrating something today?" Lisa gestured toward the bakery box on the counter.

Once she had the steak tips safely in the fridge, Maddie

replaced the full cup with an empty one and hit the brew button. "No. I didn't feel like baking anything to go with dinner, so I picked up something while I was out."

"You can't go wrong with something from Sugar and Spice."

She agreed 100 percent, and she'd had trouble deciding on a dessert. "That's why I got a Boston cream pie that's in the fridge and those cookies."

"Is Keith coming by for dinner?"

Maddie wouldn't be going through all this work just for herself. Nodding, she added sugar to her coffee. "He's helping one of our friends move into his girlfriend's house. Keith wanted me to help too. I promised to have dinner ready when he came home instead."

It happened so quickly Maddie wasn't sure if Lisa frowned at the word home or if she'd imagined it.

"I don't blame you. Moving sucks. I don't want to do it anytime soon."

Lisa sipped the coffee that she'd added so much cream and sugar to that it must taste like coffee ice cream—a flavor Maddie had only tried recently while in Maine and had instantly added to her favorite flavors list.

"Unfortunately, cooking won't get me out of helping Keith when he moves his stuff here."

Lisa's jaw clenched for the briefest of moments, and her eyes slightly narrowed. Or at least Maddie thought she saw the change.

"If he's going to be back soon, I can leave."

"No need for you to go. He'll text me before they head over to the storage facility." But Maddie wanted the conversation to move along. "You said you need to talk. Is everything okay?"

Lisa's sigh would've knocked over a small child, but rather than answer, she took another drink of her coffee. "I've been communicating with my ex-boyfriend, Tobias, for the past few weeks. I told you about him."

While not unheard of, it wasn't a currently popular name in

the US, and Maddie would have remembered if Lisa had mentioned anyone named Tobias. But in the short time Maddie had known the woman, Lisa had dated a couple of different men, so Maddie could understand how Lisa thought she had told her about him.

"Sorry, I don't remember what you told me."

"He's the *science fiction* fan." She brought the cup to her lips again.

Sharing that she'd dated someone who liked science fiction wasn't telling Maddie about the man precisely. But Maddie would not contradict her. "Oh, yeah, I remember. Is it safe to assume Teddy doesn't know?"

She'd never met Teddy, Lisa's newest boyfriend, but she had heard all about how great he was in bed.

"No, but he wouldn't care. We're only together for the sex."

Maddie couldn't imagine such an arrangement but to each their own.

A thoughtful smile spread across Lisa's face. "Tobias is my soul mate."

Outside of books, she'd heard no one refer to a person as their soul mate. "What happened between you two, then?"

"Tobias said it wasn't working out between us." Lisa gulped some coffee and then placed the cup back on the table. "But I know he didn't mean it. He just got nervous. You know how guys can get."

At least to Maddie, it sounded as if Lisa's ex didn't share her opinion about them being soul mates. But hey, if Lisa wanted to believe they were, she could.

"Can I have another cup?" Lisa removed her purse from her chair and unzipped it.

All the cream Lisa added must have cooled the coffee down considerably because she'd seen no one finish a cup of hot coffee so quickly.

"Of course." How could she say no? "I got some red velvet

white chocolate chip cookies at Sugar and Spice. Do you want one?"

She'd been itching to eat one since she walked out of the bakery. And nothing went better with coffee than a cookie or two.

"Why not?"

Maddie's cell chimed as she waited for Lisa's coffee to finish brewing. She suspected it was Alex wanting to know what Keith's answer had been last night, because unless they'd enlisted Superman's help, there was no way the guys had already finished up at Salty's house.

Coffee and bakery box in hand, Maddie turned. "Does he—"

While Maddie might have imagined Lisa frowning earlier, she wasn't imagining the look of hate on Lisa's face now or the gun in her hand.

Regardless of whether Lisa had experience with firearms was irrelevant at this distance. If Lisa pulled the trigger, a bullet would strike Maddie somewhere. And since Maddie's Glock remained locked in the safe where she kept it whenever at home, she had no way of defending herself.

But would Lisa do it?

Pointing a gun at someone was one thing. Pulling the trigger and shooting a living human was another. And while people thought they could shoot someone, it often turned out they couldn't. Unfortunately, there was no way of telling which category Lisa fell into. All Maddie could do was hope her so-called friend fell into the second.

Maddie considered and immediately dismissed tossing the hot coffee at Lisa. While it might distract her momentarily, it might also piss her off. And it was never a good idea to anger an unhinged individual who had a gun pointed at you.

If she got Lisa talking, though, maybe she'd lower the weapon. Whether or not it worked, it might give Maddie time to come up with some way to avoid having a 9mm bullet lodged in her body. Or worse, for Keith to come home and find himself on the receiving end of Lisa's gun.

"What's this about?"

Maddie ruled out a robbery attempt. If the woman wanted any money or jewelry in the house, she would've pulled out the weapon when she walked inside. Had she helped put someone Lisa cared about in prison while working for the FBI? Over the summer, someone had gone after Kenzie because her dad had sent him to prison. Or was this somehow related to an assignment she'd worked for Elite Force?

"You."

Not much of an answer.

"I don't understand, Lisa. I thought we were friends."

Slowly, Maddie set the cookies and coffee on the table. Two free hands might not make a difference, but it couldn't hurt either.

"If we'd met under different circumstances, maybe we could've been."

Judging by the sincerity in her voice, Maddie guessed Lisa believed what she said. However, her response still didn't explain why the woman stood in Maddie's kitchen pointing a gun at her.

"We still can be. Put away the gun, and I'll forget I saw it." Maddie doubted Lisa would comply, but it was worth a try.

"It's too late."

Maddie's cell beeped, telling her she'd received another text message. She should've put the device in her pocket when she left the table. Then maybe she could activate the SOS emergency feature and get some help.

"I don't believe that, Lisa. You have done nothing illegal yet." Well, except point a gun at her, but Maddie would say whatever she had to right now.

"It's your own fault, you know," Lisa said, her voice laced with bitterness. "If you'd stayed away from Keith, I wouldn't have to do this." She took a step forward, but unfortunately, she kept the gun pointed at Maddie. "I tried to get you to leave him, but you refused."

Well, that explains the why.

Maddie remembered Keith dating someone named Lisa sometime in the early spring. When she'd become friends with the woman now pointing a gun at her, Maddie never considered she was the same person.

"I—"

"You should've walked away when I sent you those pictures. He doesn't love you. Keith loves me. He's been using you to make me jealous."

The woman had so many wires crossed in her brain, who knew what she might accept at this point?

"Hey, I believe you. And I don't want to be with someone who doesn't love me. I'll call Keith now and tell him we're through. Then you guys can be together."

Shaking her head, Lisa pulled the trigger.

Click.

During her training at Quantico, Maddie's firearms instructors often said that the loudest sound someone could hear was the click of a firing pin striking without the loud bang that followed. There were many reasons it could happen, but the exact cause was not important right now. Her instructors had drilled it into her during firearms training that as soon as you heard that click, you should tap the magazine to be sure you'd inserted it correctly. Then vigorously rack the slide to put a new round in the chamber so you would be ready to fire again. Maddie and any other well-trained person could do this in under a second.

Instead of doing any of that, though, Lisa stared at the gun, confusion etched on her face. Evidently, Lisa wasn't familiar with firearms.

Get two hands on the gun.

Lunging forward, Maddie grabbed the pistol barrel with one and Lisa's wrist with the other. Using the full force of her lunge,

Maddie drove the pistol into Lisa's face and pushed her back until her body hit the wall behind her. Not losing her momentum, Maddie drove her knee into Lisa's bladder, causing her to double over in pain. Then, maintaining control over the pistol, Maddie violently twisted it, pointing the barrel directly back at Lisa and breaking her grip on the gun.

As she took two significant steps back, Maddie tapped the bottom of the magazine and racked the pistol's slide, holding it back just long enough to see that the gun chamber had been empty the entire time, and watched as a live round entered the chamber.

FIFTEEN

Keith walked backward into Kenzie's living room and hoped the bookcase he and Connor had carried over from Salty's house wasn't going upstairs. "Where do you want this?"

"Against the wall between the two windows." Salty gestured toward the far wall before taking a swig of water.

Good.

He'd been working nonstop since arriving and gone up and down so many stairs he'd be doing it in his dreams tonight. And before he moved another box or piece of furniture, he wanted a drink and something to eat.

Bookcase in place, Keith headed straight for the kitchen. "This would've gone a hell of a lot faster if you'd started moving your shit here before today," he called.

"What kind of friend would I be if I'd deprived you of having so much fun?" Salty asked, following him to the other room.

Obviously, Kenzie knew them well because she'd loaded her kitchen table with all kinds of junk food. There wasn't a single piece of fruit or even a granola bar in sight.

Biting into a double-chocolate glazed donut, Keith grabbed a water bottle from the cooler. He loved beer as much as the next guy, but it didn't go well with donuts. "Remember that when you're helping me do this in a couple of weeks."

"You're moving?" Salty grabbed two peanut butter cookies off the plate and stuffed one in his mouth. "Where to?"

"Where do you think, Ryan?" Kenzie asked, joining them in the kitchen. "Maddie's house. Right?"

"That's the plan. My lease doesn't end until January, so I've got time. But I'm going to start moving stuff when Spike and I get back from babysitting Bond."

"I don't know why the hell we got stuck with him again," Spike said around a mouthful of food.

"You two seem to be assigned to him more than any of us. I wonder if Bond asks for you guys."

Keith hadn't thought much about it, but Salty was right. This trip would be Bond's ninth to Venezuela this year and the fifth time he and Spike had gone with him. Far more than anyone else on the team.

"If you're feeling left out, I can ask Ax to send you in my place," Spike said. "I don't mind."

"And deprive you of Bond's delightful company? What kind of friend would I be if I did that?" Salty grinned and shook his head. "I couldn't do that to you. Besides, if Bond requested you and Keith, that's who he wants. And Coleman's all about keeping clients happy."

"If Bond spends more time around you, I think you'll become his new favorite person. And the next time I'm in the office, I'm going to suggest to Ax that he assign you and Connor to Bond the next time he travels. Spike, you should do the same." Keith hoped to see Lyle's name on the screen as he pulled his ringing cell phone from his back pocket.

About an hour ago, Lyle had replied to Keith's text asking him to find out what he could about the phone number he'd received the message from earlier. Lyle had promised to do what he could when he got home and get back to Keith with whatever he learned.

"Hey, Lyle. What do you have for me?"

All conversations in the room stopped.

"The number came back to a Lisa Mayfield. Her address is 55 Old Marsh Road in Dumfries."

Damn it. Spike was right.

When Lisa had stopped calling, he'd hoped she'd moved on. However, the messages and videos proved otherwise, and now he needed a plan for dealing with her. "Thanks, Lyle. I owe you one."

"I've got more for you."

Keith needed nothing else from him unless Lyle had a solution. But the guy had done him a big favor, so he'd hear him out.

"She's near Maddie's house. Or at least her phone was five minutes ago."

When Maddie had mentioned she'd grabbed dinner with Alex and someone named Lisa at Murphy's Thursday night, he hadn't found it odd. He didn't know all of Maddie's friends, and Lisa was a common name.

Coincidences happened. But not this time. Keith didn't know how or when it happened, but Maddie and Lisa knew each other.

"Thanks again. Anything you need, Lyle, just ask."

"Did Lyle get a name?" Spike asked.

Nodding, Keith sent Maddie a text. "You were right. It's the actress I dated in the spring. And I think Lisa's at Maddie's now."

Salty lowered the cookie he'd been about to bite into. "Back it up. The woman who's been sending you porn is hanging out with Mad Dog?"

"Wait, what? Someone has been sending you porn, Keith?" Kenzie asked.

Come on, Maddie, answer me.

"The answer to both questions is yes. Salty can fill you in later." It surprised Keith that Salty hadn't already told his girlfriend about it.

Maddie's plans today included shopping, cooking, and reading. She should be answering him.

Fuck, something isn't right.

While the reason she wasn't answering could be something as simple as she was in the bathroom and her phone was in the kitchen, his gut told him otherwise. "I've got to go."

"I'll go with you."

Backup was always a good idea, so he wouldn't turn down Spike's offer.

Maddie, are you home?

He sent another message before pulling away from the curb.

Assuming one drove at the speed limit, Salty lived about ten minutes away. Now wasn't the time for obeying the law. And a few minutes later, Keith parked across from Maddie's neighbor. The metallic blue two-door parked in Maddie's driveway answered his question about whether Maddie had company. And he knew who that company was because he'd been in that car.

"How do you want to handle this?"

He'd seen nothing to suggest Lisa had a violent side. But Maddie still hadn't answered his two messages or the one Spike sent her on the drive over.

"Go around the left side of the house and into the backyard."

The two most likely places for Maddie and Lisa to be were the kitchen and living room. Fortunately, neither of those rooms had windows on the left side of the house, so neither woman would see anyone approaching.

"There's a key in the thermometer mounted on the shed. Text me when you're in place."

Not wanting to alert anyone to his presence yet, Keith closed the truck door enough so a passing vehicle wouldn't take it off and switched his phone to vibrate.

Rather than walk down and cross in front of Maddie's, they headed for her neighbor's house. While Spike jumped the four-foot fence separating Maddie's yard from Declan and Robert's,

Keith kept close to the house and crouched down low as he made his way toward the front steps.

Seven-inch windowpanes flanked the front door. While they looked nice and allowed in sunlight, he viewed them as security risks. If someone wanted inside, they could break them and easily reach inside to unlock the door.

Today they allowed him to look inside while avoiding the larger windows in the living room, and the house's open floor plan meant he could see everything except the bedrooms and bathroom.

He'd envisioned a handful of scenarios since Lyle told him Lisa might be with Maddie. But none of them came close to the scene in the kitchen.

Although she'd cut and dyed her hair, there was no mistaking the woman Maddie held at gunpoint.

His cell phone vibrated, and Keith checked the screen.

?

Keith didn't need help to interpret the message. Spike saw what he did and wanted to know how Keith wished to proceed.

Maddie would expect him to come through the front. If anyone opened the back door, it might distract her. Based on the blood flowing from Lisa's nose, there had already been a struggle. He couldn't tell if Maddie was injured, and he didn't want her involved in another struggle, especially when there was at least one weapon involved.

Front only. Call 911.

While he went inside and helped Maddie, Spike could contact the authorities because this was only ending one way: with Lisa wearing handcuffs while in a police vehicle.

"You bitch. You broke my nose."

Lisa's shrill scream reached him when he opened the door. Even at this distance, he wished for some hearing protection; poor Maddie stood mere feet away from her.

"Keith will make you pay when he sees what you did."

Somehow Lisa got her voice to go an octave higher. Keith wondered if Maddie's hearing would ever be the same.

If Maddie saw him in her peripheral vision or had heard him open the door, she gave no indication. Lisa was another story.

"Keith, thank God you're here." She briefly glanced at the door he'd left open before turning her attention back to him. "She's crazy. You've got to help me," she begged.

He wanted to ask if Lisa had looked in a mirror lately because she was the only crazy person in the room. But he wanted to defuse the situation, not make it worse.

"Maddie's going to kill me because she wants to keep us apart. I told her that you love me." As if she had an on/off switch, tears filled her eyes and slipped down her face. "But she doesn't believe me. She thinks you love her."

"Lisa, Maddie isn't going to hurt you." Keith spoke as if a child stood there instead.

"She broke my nose. She is pointing a gun at me. If you hadn't walked in, she would've shot me."

"I don't think it's broken. I'll get you some paper towels for the blood."

He'd spent so much time around weapons, he could identify handguns while half asleep, and the one in Maddie's hand was a Sig. Maddie only owned a Glock, which meant Lisa had arrived with it. If she came with a gun, she might have another weapon concealed.

Lisa pounded her fist against the wall behind her. "I don't care about the blood. I want you to tell her the truth. Tell her we're going to spend our lives together and that you were using her to make me jealous."

Calm her down.

Keith slowly walked toward Lisa and pressed some towels into her left hand as he reached for her right. "Yeah, of course, we are, Lisa."

He gave Maddie the signal to lower the weapon as he

escorted Lisa to a chair. "Come on. Let's sit down, and I'll tell Maddie about our plans."

Over the past few weeks and today, Lisa's actions had proved how unstable she was. He didn't want her suddenly lunging at Maddie or making a run for the door, so he kept his hand wrapped around hers even after they sat down.

Keep her talking.

He had to keep her there until the cops arrived. Then she'd be their problem.

Keith couldn't capture her other hand, since she held the paper towel against her nose. So instead, he wrapped his left hand around her wrist and said the first thing that came to mind. "Maddie, everything Lisa said is true."

He glanced at Maddie long enough to give her a quick once-over. Her standard, neat ponytail was destroyed, but otherwise, she appeared unharmed.

"I've only been with you because I wanted to make Lisa jealous. Lisa's going to move in with me soon." Smiling, he looked back at Lisa. "Aren't you?"

Lisa nodded.

"Do you want to do it before Thanksgiving or after?"

"Before," Lisa replied, her voice back to a normal volume.

"That's what I was leaning toward too. I'll ask some friends to help us next weekend. After today, they owe me. And soon Lisa and I are going to get married."

Keith rubbed his thumb across Lisa's palm and searched his brain for something she'd want to hear. "Last week, I picked up the ring I had made for you."

Her eyebrows scrunched together, and she moved the paper towel away from her nose. "You did?"

"Of course. I don't want you wearing the same engagement ring as thirty other women. You deserve something unique." He'd thought that in terms of Maddie, but he'd use the sentiment now if it would help.

"What does it look like?"

You had to ask.

"It's a combination of white and yellow gold," he said, picturing the ring his dad had given Mom for their fortieth wedding anniversary. "There's one large square diamond on top and several round ones set in the band." He didn't know how to describe the intricate design of the band, so he wasn't even going to try.

Outside, he heard car doors close, and he tightened his hold on her hand and wrist. If the cops were about to walk in, he didn't want her making a run for the back door when she saw them.

"How many carats?"

The cops walked inside before he came up with a number.

When she spotted them, Lisa bolted out of her chair and lunged at him. "You liar. You were just trying to distract me. I'm going to kill you and then her."

ENTERING THE KITCHEN, Maddie grabbed a cookie from the bakery box still on the table. As expected, the police had wanted detailed statements from both of them and Spike. Although they'd probably only been at the station for about two hours, it had felt like forever.

"Give me a few minutes, and then I'll start dinner." Maddie bit into a cookie as she selected a bottle of wine from the fridge. An encounter with a crazy ex-girlfriend didn't cancel out the need for food.

"You don't have to cook. I can order takeout. Just tell me what you want, and I'll get it."

Keith's ex-girlfriend had already ruined much of her day. But she wouldn't let Lisa ruin her plans for tonight's meal too. "Not happening. The steak tips have been marinating, and it won't take me long to get the potatoes ready." So they could eat sooner, though, she'd skip the twice-baked potatoes and make mashed instead.

"Whatever you want to do is fine with me. Is there anything I can help with?"

She appreciated the offer, but if Keith helped, it would only create more work for her. "Yeah, get us some wineglasses."

Although they'd spoken to the police at the house and given statements at the station, they hadn't discussed what had happened today. "How did you know to come home?"

"Lisa made a mistake and used her cell phone to send me a message. Lyle did what he does best and discovered who the number belonged to and where the phone was. When you didn't answer me, I knew something was wrong."

She'd gotten the gun away from Lisa, but the situation could have still gone terribly wrong. However, Keith's arrival helped resolve it in a nonlethal fashion. "I'll have to thank Lyle later."

"I'm guessing she was following me and saw us together. But how did you get to be friends with her?" Keith asked.

"We met at the gym. And you know, at least initially, she didn't want to kill me, just convince me to leave you." Then, after filling both wineglasses and taking a sip from one, she handed Keith the other. "I don't know who the woman was, but Lisa was behind the encounter at Murphy's when I was in New York. She sent me the pictures, hoping I'd believe you were cheating on me and end things."

"She kept the crazy hidden well when I was with her. So when Spike suggested Lisa was sending the messages, I told him there was no way. I'm still having a hard time wrapping my head around it."

"Why did he think it might be her?"

"We'd only been seeing each for a little more than a month, and she wanted to move in with me. And she constantly called me after I told her it wasn't working. I thought she was just clingy. Then when she stopped, I guessed she was with someone else."

"More like obsessed. Lisa said the two of you were soul mates."

Despite the conversation topic, Keith grinned. "Soul mates? That's funny."

"Before I find myself stuck in another version of *Fatal Attraction*, do you have any other crazy ex-girlfriends who consider you their soul mate running around?"

"I think you're safe. But if anyone comes to mind, I'll let you know."

The first glass of wine finished; Maddie refilled it before opening the bag of potatoes. If they were going to eat at a reasonable time, she needed to start cooking. "Maybe you should quit working with me and go into acting. I almost believed everything you said to Lisa."

"I took drama sophomore year. Guess it paid off."

She learned new things about him all the time. "You took drama in high school?"

Keith shrugged. "I wanted an easy class. It turned out to be a lot more work than I expected. But I managed an A- for the year. The teacher wanted me to try out for the lead role in the drama club's play that year."

"Taking a class because you thought it would be an easy one sounds like something you'd do."

"Right, like you never did it?"

"Unless you count gym, which everyone had to take, the easiest class I had in high school was oral communications." She dropped the peeled potato in a pot of water and started on another.

"I took an oral communications class senior year with the teacher from hell. Everyone hated Mrs. Bell."

"I had one of those for Algebra. No one wanted to see Mr. Steward's name on their class schedule." Regardless of geographic location or size, every high school had at least one teacher everyone disliked. "When it was on, I never watched *Precinct 3*, but Lisa's a talented actress."

"Yeah, she played the role of normal well." Keith drank the last mouthful in his glass and reached for the wine bottle.

"You're not wrong there, but I was thinking about how I believed we were friends. Not once did I suspect anything. Even when she conveniently got those pictures of you, I didn't think she had an ulterior motive."

"Coleman's got contacts everywhere. I'm sure he could arrange to get her nominated for an Oscar."

"If anyone could make that happen, it'd be Coleman." The director was on a first-name basis with everyone from heads of state and CEOs to movie directors. "This will sound nuts, but I feel sorry for her."

"She tried to shoot you in your own damn kitchen." Setting down his glass, Keith pressed his palm against her forehead. "You don't feel hot. Did you bang your head trying to get the gun away from Lisa?"

Next time she'd know to keep her big mouth shut. "Really? I forgot she pointed a gun at me. What would I do without you here to remind me?" Maybe Lisa didn't deserve any sympathy, but that didn't change how Maddie felt. "She believed you loved her and couldn't accept that you'd moved on. Can you imagine being so jealous of anyone that you'd try to kill them? A person willing to go that far has mental health issues."

"No one would disagree that Lisa's got issues. Whatever attorney represents her will use an insanity defense in court."

Lisa faced a list of various charges, including attempted murder and stalking. When her day came in court, Maddie would have to see her again, but until then, she didn't want to think about her. "She's not our problem, and I don't want to waste any more time talking about Lisa tonight."

"You won't get an argument from me."

SIXTEEN

Nine Months Later

FROM HER SEAT, Maddie watched Salty and his niece dancing while Kenzie danced with the young boy who'd been their ring bearer. At some point, Kenzie had told her which of Salty's cousins the little boy belonged to, but she didn't remember which one. The guy had too many cousins for her to remember them all. She wondered if Salty even knew all their names. The presence of the children at tonight's wedding was just one of the many ways it differed from Connor and Becca's earlier this month. The other noticeable difference was the number of guests. Connor and Becca's wedding hadn't been a small affair. They both knew too many people for that. But compared to this one, though, it'd been an intimate event. Maddie hadn't done a headcount, but she estimated close to a hundred and fifty people filled the ballroom tonight. And she knew the couple hadn't invited everyone they wanted. Over lunch earlier in the summer, Kenzie shared they'd gone through the guest list multiple times and removed whomever they could to bring down the cost. At the time, she'd joked that Kenzie should either consider looking for a guy who came from a smaller family or elope.

As lovely as both weddings had been, neither was what Maddie wanted. Nope, when she and Keith got married, she wanted as few people there as possible. And while she enjoyed dancing as much as the next person, she didn't want a reception like this. Instead, she'd rather go straight on her honeymoon after they said "I do" and then have a cookout at the house when they returned.

"Whatever you do, please don't get married in the next couple of months." Alex put down her drink and retook her seat.

"You don't like weddings?"

"They're fine. But this is the fourth one I've been to this year. I need a break."

"Don't worry; I won't be inviting you to something like this anytime soon." Or hopefully ever, if Keith agreed to what she had in mind.

"Doubt that. Keith's going to ask you soon."

Alex was closer to the truth than she realized. Last week, she'd come home in time to hear Keith tell his sister he'd planned to ask her before they left for their vacation. Maddie didn't know if he'd shared any plans about how he intended to do it, because she slipped back out the door, so Keith wouldn't realize she'd overheard him. Then she'd re-entered, making as much noise as possible so Keith realized he was no longer alone.

"And he's not the type to want a long engagement. I'd guess he'd be willing to wait three or four months."

Once Keith made up his mind, his ability to wait went out the window. "I don't know even half this many people, and if I did, I wouldn't want something like this." Maddie searched the room for Keith. He'd gone to get them drinks from the bar, and she'd rather he not overhear her and Alex's conversation.

"That makes two of us." Alex raised her glass as if making a toast.

"I...." Maddie stopped when she spotted Keith walking back

toward their table. Until Keith proposed, she didn't want him to know what she had in mind.

"What was that?" Alex asked.

Maddie inclined her head in Keith's direction. "Later."

"Sorry, it took so long. The line was long." Keith handed her a glass of white wine before pulling his chair out and sitting down.

With Keith back at the table, Maddie and Alex couldn't resume their conversation, so she latched on to the first thing she saw. At the moment, it was Megan, Kenzie's maid of honor. Kenzie considered the woman more a sister than a cousin, and she'd been thrilled when Megan moved to Virginia and rented Salty's house the previous December.

"Neil's got it bad. I don't think he's danced with anyone but Megan tonight."

"No, he danced with Salty's grandmother."

"She doesn't count. Keith and Spike danced with her too, and now she's out there with Matt." Although probably in her eighties, Mrs. Russo had done more dancing than Maddie. "And speaking of men, Adam is walking this way, and he's not looking at me."

Since Adam lived in North Carolina, Maddie didn't know Salty's identical twin well, but according to Kenzie, the two men were like night and day in most ways.

"Would you like to dance?" Adam asked, turning his attention to Alex after greeting everyone.

"I'd love to."

Sipping her drink, Maddie watched the couple walk away.

"When I got the drinks, I noticed a garden outside." Keith's leg repeatedly brushed against hers as it bounced up and down. "I don't know about you, but I could use some fresh air."

She wouldn't mind a break from the music and the constant hum of various conversations. "Sounds good to me."

Shades of purple, pink, and red dominated the garden located off the hotel's main ballroom, and in the middle, a white gazebo took center stage. Both wooden and granite benches provided visitors with different places to sit and enjoy the nature around them. And for those who visited after sunset or when clouds blocked the sun like now, lights resembling small lanterns lined the walkways.

"I'm surprised there aren't other people out here." Unless people were hiding behind the larger shrubs, they had the garden to themselves.

"Maybe they're afraid to get wet."

So far, the rain had held off, but the meteorologist predicted some crazy weather would move in at some point. If anyone doubted it, all they had to do was look up at the dark clouds moving in.

"The sky doesn't look promising."

"We won't stay out here long," Keith promised as they walked down one path toward the gazebo. Like the ones along the ground, the tiny lights strung in the gazebo were on, giving it an almost magical aura.

Almost as soon as they sat inside, the door to the building opened, and a hotel employee headed their way.

"Here's the champagne you ordered." The man placed a tray containing a wine bucket and two glasses down next to Keith. "When you're finished, leave everything here, and someone will get it later."

"Champagne. What are we celebrating?" Maddie watched Keith open the bottle and pour the bubbly liquid into the glasses.

"Our anniversary."

"That's not today. It's tomorrow."

Shaking his head, Keith handed her a glass. "Tomorrow marks one year since our first date. I don't consider that our anniversary. To me, it's the night we kissed in your kitchen. Did you forget about that?"

"No." She rolled the stem of the glass between her fingers. "Both Jasmine and Cassidy called me a few days later, complaining because you'd turned them down. Before you, I don't think any guy had ever done that to either of them."

"Third-best decision I ever made."

"Do I want to know what the first ones were?"

"Number two was following you inside the house that night."

Keith reached inside his suit jacket, and even before his hand emerged, Maddie knew what she'd see when it did.

"Asking you to marry me is number one."

She rarely looked at jewelry, but she'd never seen an engagement ring like the one Keith held. Leaf-accented vines in yellow gold and two rows of aquamarines, her birthstone, wrapped around a round diamond set in white gold.

"What do you say?"

"I didn't hear you ask me anything." Occasionally, being difficult was fun.

As she expected, Keith frowned. "Madison Dempsey, will you marry me?"

"How does next Saturday sound?"

"As in a week from now?"

He'd never given an indication he wanted something like the wedding going on inside, but maybe he did.

They'd enjoyed their trip to the island so much in December that they'd booked another trip for this summer, and they were leaving next weekend. "Instead of going to Puerto Rico on Saturday, we could fly out to Vegas and get married. Then on Sunday, we head to Puerto Rico as planned. When we come home, we can have a party or maybe a cookout with our family and friends."

She'd already looked into the cost of flying to Vegas and changing their tickets to Puerto Rico. Although not an insignificant amount, doing what she had in mind would be a hell of a lot cheaper than planning a traditional wedding, even if it was smaller than this one.

Keith slipped the ring on her finger. Either he'd used something from her jewelry box to get it appropriately sized, or he'd been lucky because it fit perfectly. "Let's do it. One thing, though. I don't want an Elvis impersonator marrying us."

"No Elvis. Promise."

I hope you enjoyed Maddie and Keith's story. Read on for excerpts from The Billionaire's Homecoming, Brett Sherbrooke and Jennifer Wallaces's story, and One Of A Kind Love.

THE BILLIONAIRE'S HOMECOMING

"Mission control to space shuttle Jen, do you read me? I repeat, do you read me?"

Jennifer Wallace blinked and looked up at her sister, Kristen. "Sorry. Did you ask me something?"

Kristen nodded and held up a tomato. "I've asked you three times if you want tomatoes on your sandwich. Where were you?"

"Thinking. And no thanks, I'll skip the tomatoes today." She should've stayed home this afternoon, but she'd thought a change of scenery and some company would keep her thoughts off her upcoming meeting.

At the counter, Kristen put the finishing touches on their lunches and then called in Bella, Jen's niece, and her friend who was over for the afternoon. "Why don't you girls eat these on the deck," Kristen said, handing each girl a paper plate. "If you're still hungry later, we have ice cream in the freezer and peanut butter cookies."

Neither girl argued, and they quickly disappeared back outside.

"Do you want to talk about whatever has you so distracted? Maybe I can help." Kristen set down their sandwiches and an unopened bag of barbecue-flavored potato chips, their favorite flavor.

There was no way Kristen or anyone else could help, but maybe talking about it would get it out of her head for a bit. "Do you remember me telling you about Brett, the man I've been exchanging letters and texts with for the past year and a half?"

"Actually, it's been almost two years. We sent the first care boxes to Keith's unit at the start of our second year as Girl Scout leaders. This September will be our fourth year," Kristen said, referring to their older brother.

Jen ground her back molars together. She loved her sister, but the woman didn't understand the concept of approximation. Even in school she'd never been able to estimate the answer to a math problem. Nope, she had to get the exact answer. Jen, as well as perhaps everyone in the family, found it Kristen's most annoying characteristic. Often they teased her about it when it reared its ugly head—like now. This afternoon, Jen ignored it. Sometimes it was easier.

"But to answer your question, yes, I remember. You've talked so much about him I feel like I know him," Kristen said.

"I'm supposed to finally meet him this week after work."

Kristen tore open the chips and added a handful to her plate before passing the bag to Jen. "In a public place I hope."

Although really her adopted sister and only six months older, Kristen had always played the role of the protective big sister. "Yes, of course. We're meeting at Ambrosia."

"Awesome. What's the problem then? You're already half in love with the man. I'd think you'd be excited about finally meeting him face-to-face."

Unfortunately, her sister's assessment wasn't far from the truth. She'd never admit Kristen was right though. Kristen's belief that she was always correct no matter the topic was her sister's second-biggest flaw.

"Well, let's see," Jen said. "To start with, I'm about to sit down and have coffee with Brett Sherbrooke. You may have heard of his family. They own this small, insignificant hotel chain, but if you haven't, I'm sure you've heard of his uncle, President Sherbrooke. You know, the man who lives in the big white house on Pennsylvania Avenue and travels in Air Force One."

Her sister's mouth opened and closed several times. She'd had a similar reaction when she finally found out just whom she'd been corresponding with for months too.

"Wait, a minute. Back up." Kristen pointed a potato chip at her. "You never told me any of this before. Does Keith know?"

Since Brett and their brother had served together, Jen guessed he knew, although Keith had never mentioned it to her. "Probably, but I never asked him. I'm not even sure Keith knows Brett and I have been communicating all this time. I never told him. Did you?"

Kristen shook her head. "Why didn't you tell me before now? I mean it's not like you never talk about the man."

"At first I only knew his first name. Later, I thought it was just a coincidence his name was Brett Sherbrooke. A lot of people have the same name. I knew a guy at Northeastern named Anderson Brady, and he wasn't the actor."

"Fair enough. But you must have learned the truth long before this month. You've been writing to him for almost two years!"

Jen toyed with the napkin near her plate and nodded. "Yeah, but when I figured it out, he was halfway across the world in some place I can't even pronounce. It didn't seem like a big deal."

"How *did* you figure it out anyway? Did he actually tell you in an e-mail or something?"

She remembered very well the moment she put it together. "Not exactly. Last year he mentioned how disappointed he was that he wasn't going to make it to Providence for his cousin Trent's wedding."

Jen could accept there was more than one man in the world

with the name Brett Sherbrooke. She couldn't accept there was more than one who also had a cousin named Trent living in Providence who was getting married.

"I see how you would've reached that conclusion. I would've too, but did you ever actually ask him? It might be a stretch, but he still might not be part of *that* Sherbrooke family."

"Oh, trust me he is. We exchanged pictures sometime last year, and I compared it to a picture I found on the internet taken at a fund-raiser a few years ago. In it he's standing with Jake and Trent Sherbrooke."

Kristen tapped her fingers on the table but didn't respond right away. While Jen waited for her sister's next question, and she knew there would be more, she started on her lunch.

Her sister's fingers stopped moving. "I'd be a little nervous too, but I don't see what the big deal is. You've never met in person, but it's not like you don't know the guy. The two of you have exchanged enough letters, e-mails, and texts to wallpaper my entire house. And you already know what he looks like, so you don't have to worry about finding some eighty-year-old man with warts waiting for you. I say relax, enjoy the afternoon, and see where things go."

Ah yes, they'd exchanged pictures, and there was the other problem that had been plaguing her thoughts ever since Brett said he was moving back to New England and would love to finally meet.

"Well, the whole picture thing is kind of part of the problem."

"I'm afraid to ask, but I will anyway," Kristen said.

Of course she would because this was her sister. And Kristen never held anything back. It was actually one of the things she loved about her. Kristen was always upfront and honest.

"Did you send him a picture of someone else?"

She'd briefly considered it, because at the time she hadn't expected to ever meet him. Kristen didn't need to know that small detail. "Of course not."

"Then what? Did you have one of those boudoir photo shoots done and then send him some sexy pictures?"

Really, Kristen knew her better than that, but evidently she wanted to give her a hard time this afternoon. "Get real. That's something you'd do and then give to Dan as a present."

"Did he tell you?" Her sister's face took on a slight pink hue.

"Your husband didn't tell me anything. But your face is right now. Did you really have one of those done?" For the moment their discussion of her upcoming meeting could take a back burner. This was way too good to pass up

The pink spread from Kristen's cheeks to her hairline, and she looked away. "I wanted to get him something different for his birthday. I'd read about them being *the thing* right now and figured what the heck. He's the only one who'll ever see them." She cleared her throat and met Jen's eyes again. "But let's get back to your story. It's more interesting."

She'd love to tease Kristen about the photo gift, but if she did, her sister would find some way to repay the favor later. "I sent Brett my favorite picture from Mom and Dad's fortieth anniversary party. You know, the one I had framed of you, me, and Keith together."

"It's a great picture of you. I don't see the problem."

"That's the problem right there. It's too good. It's not the real me. Before the party, we both went to the salon and had someone do our hair and makeup. Before he printed the picture, the photographer removed any blemishes. I never look the way I do in that photo." It was one of the reasons she'd had it framed in the first place.

Kristen waved a dismissive hand in her direction. "Jennifer, you're being absolutely ridiculous. You never wear your hair the way you did to the party, but otherwise you don't look any different in the picture than you normally do."

She had a mirror at home, and the reflection greeting her every morning did not resemble the person in the picture she'd sent Brett. Unfortunately, there wasn't much she could do about it now. So the way she saw it, she had two options: either meet Brett this week at Ambrosia, or cancel altogether. But canceling their meeting would probably also mean she'd have to stop corresponding with him—something she didn't want to do.

"I'm still not sure I should go."

"Come on, be serious. What's the worst thing that could happen? You talk and then you go home alone and never hear from him again. Truthfully, I don't see that happening. Not after all this time."

She couldn't argue with Kristen's logic. Her life wouldn't end if their meeting didn't go well. She'd be disappointed though, because like her sister said, she was already half in love with the man.

"And if it does happen, well, his loss, not yours. Besides, who knows, you might spend five minutes with the man and decide he's the biggest jerk who ever lived." Kristen touched her hand and gave it a squeeze. "Jen, go. Drink some coffee, talk, and see what happens."

Just because they'd never met face-to-face didn't mean she didn't know Brett well enough to know he wasn't a jerk.

"What's it going to be, sis? Finally meet the potential love of your life, or help me take Bella and her friends to their first concert. It's not sold out; I can still get you a ticket. I'll even order it before you leave today."

She loved her niece, but she had no desire to take Bella and her friends to their first concert. "Tough one. I can either have coffee with a gorgeous man or help supervise a group of nine- and ten-year-old girls." Jen pretended to weigh both options with her hands. "Thanks for the offer, sis, but this time I'll go the gorgeous man route."

***

Brett followed the GPS directions and took a left. Sprawling estates lined both sides of the street. He'd visited his cousin

Callie's home in Connecticut only once despite numerous invites in the past. He hadn't planned on visiting today, but a stop there now would help break up his ride from Virginia to Massachusetts—a trip he'd started over eleven hours ago. And assuming he didn't hit any more traffic, he still had another three and a half hours to look forward to. Delays through Maryland and New Jersey had already tacked on several extra hours in the car, and he didn't know how much more he could handle. A short visit at his cousin's house would give him a chance to relax, stretch his legs, and hopefully avoid any weekend backups on the Mass Turnpike.

"You have arrived. Your destination is on the right," the GPS informed him.

After turning, he approached the security gate and pressed the intercom.

"Can I help you?" a male voice asked

"I'm here to see Callie and Dylan," Brett answered.

"Name, please."

"Brett."

"I'm sorry, there is no Brett on the guest list. I'll have to check with the Talbots."

Guest list? Damn, were Callie and Dylan having a party? "I'm her cousin," he added, not that he expected the individual to open the gate without speaking to either his cousin or her husband first.

"One moment please."

The intercom went silent, and Brett considered calling Callie rather than wait for whoever had answered to find her in the house. Before he got the chance, the gates opened. He didn't wait for any further invitation.

He drove down the long, winding driveway. When he reached the house, he found several other cars already parked there. The only one he recognized was his brother's car. All the others had out-of-state plates though, and since two were from Rhode Island, two were from Virginia, and another from New

York, he assumed several of his family members were visiting. With so many relatives here, Brett had a feeling he'd be there longer than he'd originally planned.

Before he had a chance to ring the doorbell, the front door opened and a petite woman stepped toward him.

"I can't believe you're here." Callie hugged him before he could manage a simple hello. "Everyone's going to be so surprised when they see you."

Brett hugged her back. "Having a party?"

"Don't worry, it's only family." She closed the door behind him as she spoke. "Well, Lauren and her husband, Nate, are here too, but they're like family."

He'd never met Callie's best friend, but he'd heard her talk about Lauren and her husband. Callie listed the other family members there as she led him through the house.

"Look who's here," she said, stepping outside before him.

All conversations stopped, and every head turned his way. Even the toddlers playing seemed to pause and look at him. Just as suddenly everyone started talking at once.

"Did you finally decide to go AWOL?" his brother, Curt, asked, coming over and giving him a hug and slap on the back.

"Nah, the Army decided they'd had enough of him and kicked him to the curb," Trent, one of his many cousins present, said, giving him a hug as well.

Brett accepted the lemonade Callie handed him and took a sip before answering. "Thought I'd stop and visit on my way home. If I'd known you two were here, I would've kept on going."

His younger brother shrugged and rejoined the woman he'd been sitting with. She'd been with Curt at Kiera and Gray's wedding in June too, although he hadn't spoken much to her. He hadn't had a chance. Before the ceremony even started, they'd left because she had an emergency at home. He hadn't spoken with his brother since then, so he didn't know what the emergency had been or how it had turned out.

"In case you don't remember him, Taylor, this grouch is my brother, Brett," Curt said to the woman next to him.

Ignoring his brother's comment, he approached Curt's girlfriend. "It's nice to see you again." Brett smiled and held out his hand.

Shaking his hand, Taylor smiled back. "Likewise."

"So where have you been?" Callie asked.

He watched the toddlers who were playing with a young girl he didn't recognize. He hadn't seen any of his cousins' children in several months, but it was easy to pick out James, Callie and Dylan's son. He had dark brown hair like Callie and Dylan, and blue-gray eyes. Figuring out which child belonged to Trent and which belonged to Jake was another story. Both had the trademark Sherbrooke blue eyes, a trait his brother possessed as well, and dirty-blond hair. It didn't help that Kendrick, Trent's son, and Garrett, Jake's son, were only three months apart in age.

"Nowhere," he answered. For the moment, he gave up trying to figure out which boy belonged to which cousin and turned his attention to the young girl. She looked to be about seven or so. Since he knew she didn't belong to any of his cousins, she had to be related to either Callie's friend Lauren or Curt's girlfriend. Curt hadn't mentioned his girlfriend had any children, but the girl didn't resemble Lauren or husband in the least either.

"Two seconds ago you said you were on your way back to Virginia," Trent said.

"He's experiencing memory problems. It happens a lot to old people," Curt said.

If not for the children present, he'd tell his brother just where he could shove his comment.

"He's not old, Curt," the unknown girl said, looking back at his brother before he could come up with a suitable non-explicit response to Curt's insult.

Taylor laughed. "Reese, Curt's only teasing his brother."

"But he is older than me," Curt added.

Mystery solved. The girl belonged with Taylor. He'd have to

ask Curt later why he hadn't told him his new girlfriend had a daughter. "Wrong. I said I was on my way home. I never mentioned Virginia."

Other than Dad, Uncle Warren, and his friend Jen, no one knew his plans. He'd held off on sharing them with anyone else, even Mom, in case something unexpected happened. With everything on track, he saw no reason to keep quiet any longer.

"Then you're going to see Mom and Dad?" Curt asked.

He hadn't thought of his parents' house as home in a long time. "No. I'm headed to North Salem," Brett answered. "I bought a house there about a year ago."

"Really?" Jake asked.

Brett thought he'd told his cousin, but evidently he hadn't. "Yeah, your brother-in-law checks on it once a month or so for me."

He'd met Sean O'Brien, Jake's brother-in-law, at his cousin's house not long after Jake got married. They'd hit it off and become friends. When he'd decided to buy a place in North Salem where both Jake's brother-in-law and mother-in-law lived, Sean had offered to check in on it and let him know if any problems developed. Thankfully, none ever had.

"Sean never said anything to me," Jake said before turning to his wife. "Did he tell you?"

Charlie shook her head. "Nope. Where in town is it?" Charlie had grown up in North Salem and made regular trips back to visit her family whenever she could.

"Union Street. Not far from the police station." Since he'd known the house would be vacant for at least a year, he'd figured owning a home virtually across the street from a police station was a bonus.

"My friend Jessie and her husband live on Union Street," Charlie said, picking up the little boy now standing near her, solving the mystery of which toddler was Jake's son.

Brett hadn't spent enough time at the house to meet any of his neighbors. In the time he'd owned it, he'd only stayed there a handful of nights, the most recent being when he'd come home for his cousin's wedding in June.

"How long are you staying up here this time?" Curt asked. "If you have time, come up and visit us. North Salem isn't far from Pelham."

"Permanently." He'd spent a fair amount of time preparing for this transition, but saying the word still felt strange.

Jake laughed at him. "Nice one. You almost had me. You went a little too far though. Everyone here knows you didn't retire from the Army. It's stuck with you for life. What are you really doing up here this weekend?"

Fair enough. Since the day he entered West Point, he'd never let on he intended to do more with his life than serve his country. And until the past two or so years, he hadn't considered it himself. "I didn't retire, but I'm no longer on active duty either. If I'm needed, they can call me up, but I don't see it happening."

"You're serious?" Curt asked, still sounding suspicious.

Brett nodded. "Affirmative. I plan to run for Senator Marshall's seat next year."

Few people knew the longtime United States Senator from Massachusetts didn't intend to run for reelection when his term ended the following year. However, since Senator Marshall happened to be good friends with his uncles and dad, he'd learned of the man's plan more than a year ago. "That's why I bought the house in North Salem when I did."

"Dad mentioned Richard wasn't going to run again," Curt said. "Half expected him to suggest I move back to Massachusetts and run for it. Not that I ever would, but we both know that wouldn't stop Dad from trying."

It was no secret Jonathan Sherbrooke still wanted his sons to follow the same path so many Sherbrooke males had been taking for years. For a long time, Dad had been content his younger son worked in the financial world at least. However, Curt's recent decision to leave his position at Nichols Investment to be a full-time author baffled the man.

"Let me see if I've got this. You're moving to North Salem and running for Richard Marshall's Senate seat next year?" Jake asked.

His cousin still didn't sound as if he believed anything Brett had told him. And Brett understood Jake's lack of acceptance. In many ways they were a lot alike. Neither had followed the path their fathers had wanted them to, and neither had ever exhibited any interest in entering politics. Trent had always been the one they expected to follow that particular Sherbrooke tradition.

"Did you take a blow to the head recently?" Curt asked before Brett answered Jake. "You detest politics."

His brother was wrong on that front. He didn't hate politics. Rather, he disliked most of the politicians serving in Washington. Brett saw that as a big distinction.

"I think it's a great idea," Callie said before Trent or another of his cousins who hadn't chimed in yet could give him a hard time too. "Let me know if I can help."

"You're serious," Curt said.

"I already have a list of potential campaign managers from Uncle Warren and Dad."

Trent and Dylan, Callie's husband, exchanged a look. "If Marty Phillips is on the list, ignore him and keep looking," Trent said.

"Trent's right," Dylan added.

He'd scanned the list quickly but didn't recall if the man had been mentioned or not. But he trusted Trent's and Dylan's judgment. If his cousin and his friend thought he should avoid Marty Phillips, he would. There were plenty of names on the list anyway.

"Anyone you recommend, Trent?" Brett asked.

Prior to his marriage, Trent had planned to run for the US Senate himself. According to Curt, their cousin had even hired a campaign manager. Before any serious campaigning could get underway, Trent had changed his mind and soon after announced his engagement. However, it wasn't a secret Trent still planned to enter politics someday.

Trent reached down and grabbed the pink plastic pig his son had sent flying under his chair. "I'd go with anyone Uncle Warren suggested except Marty Phillips," he answered, handing the toy back to Kendrick, who walked back to the farmhouse he was playing with.

He'd look over the list, talk to Dad and maybe his uncles too, and do some research. It wasn't like he had to make a decision this week or anything.

***

Although he found spending time with his family enjoyable, he was anxious to get home. So when Callie invited him to spend the night, he turned down her offer. Pulling over for a second time since leaving her house, he wished he hadn't. The rain had started the moment he crossed the Connecticut–Massachusetts border. At first it had been little more than a soft drizzle. It had quickly changed to a downpour as the winds picked up. A dazzling lightning storm soon followed. He'd been forced to pull over into the breakdown lane the first time visibility became nonexistent, outside of Grafton. He'd sat there for a solid ten minutes before the rain let up enough to see again.

Brett switched on the car's hazard lights, although considering the visibility out there, he didn't think any approaching vehicles would even see them. Picking up his cell phone, he opened the weather app. He didn't like what he saw. According to the screen, the storm was moving toward North Salem rather than away from it. He'd be dealing with it the rest of his trip home.

He'd heard his cell phone beep while driving. Pulled over for the moment anyway, he checked the text message.

Call me as soon as you get a chance. The message from Dad immediately sent up red flags.

Dad never asked him to call, and they already had plans to meet this week. If Dad was requesting a call tonight, something must be wrong. He'd seen Nana less than two months ago at his cousin's wedding. She'd looked as healthy and energetic as always despite her advanced years. Had something happened to her or Mom?

Before calling, he checked his watch. It was close to one in the morning. If he called back now, he risked waking his parents. Instead he hit reply and typed back a message. If Dad remained awake, he'd answer, and if not, he'd try again later in the morning. Brett held the phone and waited.

The rain pounding the windshield gradually subsided, and Brett could once again see the road. Tossing the cell phone onto the passenger seat, he got back underway. No reply from Dad either meant the man was asleep or too busy. He'd have to wait to find out what was going on and hope everyone he cared about was okay.

End of excerpt from The Billionaire's Homecoming.

ONE OF KIND LOVE

NOT AGAIN. ISABELLE MARTIN LOOKED AT THE TEXT MESSAGE and the attached screenshot of the schedule from Heather, her future sister-in-law, and counted to ten before she responded. It was the second time this week Heather had sent her almost exactly the same message. While she recognized that her twin brother's fiancée meant well, she didn't need the woman to send her even one copy of the ferry schedule, never mind two. Unlike Bryson's fiancée, Isabelle had lived most of her life on Sanborn Island, and she knew exactly how many times each day the ferry left Portsmouth, New Hampshire, for the island in the summer and vice versa. And since the ferry had been operating on the same schedule for at least the past twenty years, she knew most of the departure and estimated arrival times as well.

"Heather again?" Ella, her cousin, asked.

Although a few years younger than Isabelle, Ella had always been not only her favorite cousin but also the sister she didn't have. Every summer growing up, Ella and occasionally Ella's older sister, Claire, would spend a large chunk of the summer with Isabelle and her family on the island. Then in the winter, Isabelle and sometimes Bryson would tag along on the Bridges' ski vacations, since their dad didn't ski and their mom hated to take time off from work unless absolutely necessary. And ever since Isabelle first started teaching at North Salem High and moved to town, they'd become permanent fixtures at each other's homes. In fact, Ella's husband, Striker, often joked that Isabelle should just sell her house and move into their spare bedroom.

Nodding, Isabelle grabbed a pair of shorts from the laundry basket and folded them before adding them to her suitcase.

"She can't help it." Ella added the T-shirt she'd folded to the suitcase before reaching for something else.

Isabelle already knew that. But it didn't make the constant text messages and phone calls from Heather reminding Isabelle of everything, even not to forget her own damn bridesmaid dress, as if she ever would, any less annoying.

"She's just excited about the wedding. You know I wasn't much better when Striker and I got married."

At least one of us is excited. Well, perhaps that wasn't entirely true. When Bryson and Heather announced their engagement last year, Isabelle had been over the moon happy for them. They'd been together for years, and she genuinely adored her brother's fiancée. Heather was the perfect woman for her twin. In fact, she couldn't have created a better match for Bryson. And if not for one particular individual on the guest list, she'd be looking forward to her brother's upcoming wedding as much as the rest of the family.

Her cousin added a pair of shorts to the suitcase and grabbed the shirt on top of the clean laundry as she continued. "Since we're talking about the wedding anyway...." Ella paused and held up the clean T-shirt a student in Isabelle's AP United States history class had given her last year, which featured Martin Luther King Jr.'s quote *We are not makers of history. We are made by history.*

"We weren't talking about Bryson and Heather's wedding, and you know it."

The last thing she needed was Ella bringing up the wedding

again. The last time one of their conversations went down that path, she'd told Ella to mind her own business and then proceeded to avoid her for three days. A rather childish move, but Isabelle had hoped it would drive home the point she didn't want to discuss the event again. And she'd rather not get into an argument with her cousin today, especially since she needed Ella to drive her to Portsmouth tomorrow so she could catch the ferry.

"Sure we were. I told you Heather couldn't help it because she's excited about the wedding, remember. Oh, and by the way, I love this shirt. I've never heard this quote, but I like it." Ella grinned and added the T-shirt to the suitcase.

"Not many people are familiar with it," Isabelle admitted.

She had more of a chance of convincing Dad he should stop being a New England Rebels football fan and start rooting for the New York Jets than she had of getting her cousin to talk about something besides the wedding—or more specifically, one particular guest who'd be at the wedding. She had her fingers crossed he'd leave right after the reception, though, so that she could enjoy some time on the island.

"Have you decided what you're wearing to the rehearsal dinner? I think you should go with the blue sundress you bought for your cruise in February. It makes the blue in your eyes stand out."

If Isabelle kept the conversation centered on her clothing options, perhaps she'd survive their conversation. "I might pack it. But I might just wear the white dress I bought last month. I'm bringing that one and the floral one I wore to your Memorial Day cookout."

Her cousin wrinkled her nose and left her spot on the bed.

"What's wrong with those two? You have one almost identical to the floral one. And you were with me when I bought the other one. Actually, you suggested I get it."

"Nothing is wrong with them. They're both just plain. Boring. Great to wear to a cookout or maybe to school but not right for this occasion," Ella answered with a shrug as she opened Isabelle's closet. "You want something that will draw attention your way."

"Did I miss the memo? Who said I want anyone's attention? This is Bryson and Heather's wedding. They're the ones everyone should be paying attention to, not me."

Her cousin looked through the various clothes hanging up. When she reached a dark red, sleeveless wrap dress, she pulled it out but quickly returned it. "Sure, during the ceremony. But the time before and after is up for grabs."

If only Isabelle had a good comeback for that comment.

"And it's not like CJ is going to be the only handsome, eligible man on the island for the wedding. I've met a lot of Bryson's friends over the years, and if I weren't married, I wouldn't mind catching the eye of several of them."

To anyone else, Ella's statement would sound both innocent and logical. Isabelle had been single for almost a year, and it'd been months since her last date. But she knew better.

"You can cut the crap, Ella. We both know you're thinking about CJ." She tossed the shorts she held into the suitcase rather than bothering to fold them.

The moment her brother and Heather announced their engagement, she'd known he would ask Cameron, aka CJ, to be his best man. Who else would he ask? Sure, Bryson had plenty of friends, some he'd even had since elementary school. None of those friendships, though, fell into the same category as his and CJ's. At one time, her friendship with CJ had been similar as well. But that had been a long time ago—before she stopped seeing him as almost a second brother and before he kissed her.

Still, she'd hoped her brother would ask maybe Adam Sinclair, his college roommate freshman and sophomore years. Or even Pierre Blanchet. Bryson had lived with Pierre's family the year he spent studying in France, and he'd stayed in contact with them ever since. In fact, Pierre, his parents, and his sister were attending Bryson's wedding next weekend.

All the finger crossing and hoping in the world hadn't mattered. And soon, she'd find herself face-to-face with Cam.

No, don't think of him as Cam.

Growing up, she'd been the only one to call him that. Everyone else had either called him CJ or simply Ferguson, so as not to confuse him with his father, Cameron Jacob Ferguson Sr. If she started thinking of him as Cam now, she'd soon find herself going down a path she didn't want to walk again.

"Maybe just a little." Ella held her index finger and her thumb less than an inch apart, as if to reinforce her statement.

Well, at least she admitted it this time.

"But your brother does have some handsome single friends, and a lot of them will be there, Iz."

She knew full well which of her brother's friends would be there. And she couldn't deny many of them were handsome as well as genuinely nice men, including Adam. Unfortunately, she wasn't and never had been interested in any of Bryson's friends except one.

"I can't argue with you there." Flopping back on the bed, she stared up at the ceiling as she once again thought about their last conversation regarding this topic. "I spent…."

"You spent what?" Ella asked when Isabelle didn't continue.

Once again, she'd opened her mouth before she fully considered the ramifications. Oh well, too late now. If she said nothing, Ella would hound her until she came clean. Unfortunately, at the moment, she couldn't think of a plausible white lie that would satisfy her cousin's curiosity.

"I spent some time thinking about your suggestion. You know, to write to the Love Vixen?"

She'd laughed when Ella first suggested the idea. While she found the popular international blog entertaining and had even bought the Love Vixen's best-selling book, *Love Like a PB&J Sammie,* she never envisioned herself writing to her. After all, who in their right mind asked a stranger for relationship advice? Not only that, how could a person give helpful answers when they didn't know the parties involved or their history? Still, she'd given her cousin's suggestion a lot of thought. Finally, she'd concluded that if she wrote into the blog and got an answer, Ella would let the matter go once and for all. Not only that, whatever answer she received might silence the nagging voice in her head that kept telling her to take Ella's advice.

"Oh. And?"

"I decided to do it. I figured what's the worst that can happen?"

While she knew some people, like Ella, read the popular blog daily, she checked it once or twice a week. She'd never read a single post that included anyone's name. Instead, people always signed with something like Cupcake Girl or Risky Business. She'd found it easy enough to come up with a cute alias of her own. She'd also made sure not to mention the name CJ Ferguson, a name known around the world these days, or hint at her location, so even Ella, one of her closest friends, would never guess the request for help came from her. That was assuming, of course, the Love Vixen answered. Considering how popular the blog had become over the past year, she could only imagine how many people wrote in daily. She doubted the Love Vixen commented on everything she received.

Ella stopped going through the dresses in the closet and zipped back to the bed. "When? Did she answer? What did she say? I bet she said the same thing I've been telling you for months."

"To answer your first question, I did it last week," Isabelle answered as she moved back into an upright position. "As for your second, I haven't checked." Honestly, she hadn't looked at the blog again all week.

"Afraid to find out I was right?"

"Just haven't gotten around to it."

"Yeah, I know you've been so busy since school ended for the summer on Wednesday, and you're on vacation until August."

So what if she'd been a tad apprehensive about checking? "It's a good thing I like you."

"You love me, and you know it, cuz. And now is as good a time as any to check." Ella reached into her back pocket. "My cell must be in the kitchen."

Before she changed her mind, Isabelle retrieved the bag she kept her laptop in and pulled the device out. She'd left it on the floor by the nightstand on Wednesday and hadn't touched it since. Then she typed the web address for the blog into the internet browser. She could've just as easily checked the site on her cell phone, but this way, they could both read the response at the same time. Assuming, of course, the Love Vixen had answered her.

Isabelle skimmed through the numerous posts looking for hers. She found it halfway down the page.

DEAR LOVE VIXEN,

I am actually writing to you for my cousin because she's too stubborn to do it herself. In a week, she's returning home for her twin brother's wedding. Unfortunately, her brother's best man, the very man who kissed her sixteen years ago and she hasn't seen since, is returning as well. I told her to make her move and finally know once and for all how he feels. She disagrees. She plans to avoid him as much as possible until he goes back to the West Coast. Should she take my advice or let him disappear from her life for another sixteen years?

SINCERELY,
A Concerned Cuz

DEAR CUZ,
Oh, sweetie, you should... I mean your "cuz" should defi-

nitely listen to your voice of reason. If she's been pining for him for sixteen years, there's obviously something there. At least for "her." You tell her LV said to go for it. What has she got to lose? Another sixteen years of wondering "what if"? Most importantly, what has she got to gain? A wonderful happily ever after.

GOOD LUCK, *hon!*
The <3 Vixen

SHE REREAD the response from the Love Vixen. Although not the exact words Ella had used when she offered her opinion, the advice was along the same lines. It also caused the nagging voice in her head to grow louder rather than silence it once and for all.

"Pretending to be me?" Ella asked, looking at her when she finished reading the blog.

She shrugged and read the next comment on the blog from someone calling themselves Falling Hard In Providence.

"At least you were honest about being stubborn." Ella nudged her in the arm and smiled. When Ella received a dirty look in response, she laughed. "Well, once again, I agree with LV's advice. I think you should listen to her."

Isabelle's eyes drifted back to the response. Whether she wanted to admit it or not, the Love Vixen made some good points. If she ignored CJ while he was on the island, she might spend another sixteen years wondering "what if." Then again, if she made her feelings known, she might find herself suffering from the worst case of embarrassment ever and avoiding CJ at all costs until the wedding and then returning to North Salem as soon as her brother said "I do" if CJ decided to stick around.

"What's it going to be, Iz? Are you going to take our advice or hide at your parents' house until CJ leaves?"

She pictured the last magazine cover she'd seen CJ on while

standing in line for a coffee. Supermodel Milan Novak had been attached to his arm as they exited a restaurant in Los Angeles. She hadn't seen any pictures of the two of them together again since, but she didn't exactly go searching the internet looking for him either.

At least not anymore.

Yeah, she wasn't proud of it, but after he'd landed his first starring movie role, she'd read every article she could find and checked the web regularly for new photos of him. But that had been a long time ago.

Slowly, the image of him and the supermodel dissolved, and the memory of the last time they'd spoken replaced it. That night he hadn't looked at her like she was his best friend's sister. For a brief time, she'd stopped being the girl he'd known all his life and had spent hours hanging around with. Instead, she'd become someone he kissed and then made a promise to—a promise he'd failed to keep, and she'd never asked him why.

Isabelle forced the memory away.

Some decisions she didn't have to make today. "Honestly, Ella, I'm not sure. But I'm packing the blue dress."

***

"What are you doing here?" Brianna asked rather than say hello when Cameron entered the living room.

"Last time I checked, I live here."

Although he had plenty of options, he sat down next to his younger sister on the sofa. Not only was Brianna his only sister, but for the past year and a half, she'd also been his personal assistant—a position he'd hired her for after she graduated college with a bachelor's degrees in art history and medieval literature and, big surprise, couldn't find a job. In addition to providing her with a paying job, Cameron had handed over the keys to the guest house on the estate, so she had a place to live. Although more times than not, he found her in his house like now.

"So maybe I should be the one asking you that question."

The empty ice-cream container on the table provided him with a likely reason for her visit. As a way to avoid eating anything unhealthy, she never kept junk food in her house. Instead, she raided his kitchen when a craving for ice cream or chips struck. She invaded his junk food stash at least once a week.

"I couldn't find anything to eat at my house. And I knew you wouldn't mind if I grabbed something here."

Cameron picked up the empty container of chocolate chip peanut butter ice cream. "That depends on whether this was the last pint or not?"

"We're leaving tomorrow. Does it really matter if there is any left?" Brianna asked, glancing up from her laptop.

"I take that to mean you ate the last of it."

When it came to junk food, he ate almost anything, but he always went for something containing peanut butter and chocolate first when it came to ice cream or cookies. As far as he was concerned, there wasn't a better combination out there. It was as if the two substances had been made for each other, and he dared anyone to disagree with him.

"There's some Rocky Road in the freezer."

Cameron grabbed the remote off the end table. "Then you should've eaten that instead," he grumbled before pressing the power button.

"It's only ice cream, CJ. I'll go get you more right now if it's that big a deal."

"I'm just giving you a hard time." He nudged her in the arm with his elbow and reminded himself his current mood had nothing to do with his sister. "Forget about it. You know you're welcome to anything in the house."

Brianna looked unconvinced, which didn't surprise him. "If you change your mind, let me know. I'll head over to the store." Her fingers moved across the keyboard, and a new screen appeared on her laptop. "What's up with you lately anyway?"

Two words answered her question—words Cameron refused to utter even to his sister. "Nothing."

"Yeah, I believe that one."

Thanks to the ten-year age difference between them, they hadn't been close growing up. But since Brianna had been working for him, that had changed, and now she knew his moods well. Maybe too well.

Setting her laptop on an end table, Brianna turned so she could see him. "I don't know how to describe you this week, but you haven't been yourself. You haven't really been yourself for over a month. But this week has been the worst. And now you're sitting at home with me on a Saturday night—your last Saturday night in California before you head home to utter boredom for at least three weeks."

Unlike his sister, who hadn't been able to leave Sanborn Island fast enough, he'd never felt a burning desire to get away from it. In fact, if he'd been able to pursue his career and remain on the island, he would've.

"You don't have to fly out with me tomorrow. Come whenever you want, then leave right after Bryson and Heather's wedding."

Although his best friend's wedding wasn't until the weekend, they were both headed to northern New Hampshire tomorrow, where they planned to spend two days visiting their aunt and uncle before taking the ferry over to Sanborn Island. At the moment, he planned to spend at least a few weeks there. But that didn't mean his sister had to as well.

"And listen to Mom complain? No, thank you. I'll leave with you tomorrow." She patted his leg affectionately. "Is a lack of sex the cause of your current mood? It has been an unusually long time since I saw a female visitor at your kitchen table in the morning."

She could spend the rest of the night guessing and never figure it out.

"Now that I think about it, when was the last time you went out at all?"

The media liked to label him a playboy. He'd earned the title too. Not that he slept with every woman he went out with, but he preferred to remain unattached. Over the past month or so, though, he'd spent most of his time either alone or hanging around with his sister, like now. And his lack of social activity was caused by the same thing putting him in a foul mood tonight.

"Since when did you become my keeper?"

"I'm your personal assistant, remember? Keeping track of your daily life and making sure you're where you're supposed to be is part of my job."

He couldn't argue with her there, but man, he wished he could. That didn't stop him from tossing a pillow at her smiling face.

"Not that it's any of your business, but I've been out." His sister didn't need to know the last time he'd gone out on a date had been three weeks ago. "And if I've been in a bad mood, it's because I'm not done with my best man speech." While not a complete lie, it wasn't the whole truth either. He'd written the speech but wanted to fine-tune it before delivering it at Bryson and Heather's reception.

"Are you serious? How hard can it be? You and Bryson have been friends forever. I'm surprised you didn't write one a long time ago, so all you needed to do when the time came was include the bride's name. I bet Bryson has one ready for when it's your turn to get married."

Despite the length of their friendship, it'd taken him several attempts before he got anything decent on paper.

Brianna shook her head before speaking again. "Now that I think about it, he probably doesn't. He knows the odds of you ever getting married are almost nonexistent."

One thing he could say about his sister, she told you what she was thinking regardless of whether you wanted to know or not.

"Too bad there isn't a best man speech blog where you can ask for help. Kind of like people do with the Love Vixen," she continued.

Not again. His sister had been obsessed with the Love Vixen blog since it debuted. She made a point to bring it up a few times a week. Perhaps he should've told her he'd been constipated all week and that was why he was grumpy instead of bringing up his speech.

"Let me guess. That's what you're reading now." He gestured toward her laptop before scrolling through the numerous channels he paid for every month and yet still could rarely find anything he wanted to watch.

With a nod, she put her laptop back on her lap. "There are some great ones today. But I think my favorite one is from A Concerned Cuz."

He couldn't blame people for using an alias when they signed their requests. If he ever wrote into a blog asking for romantic advice—or any kind of advice, for that matter—he wouldn't use his actual name either.

"I think the person who wrote it is the one who wants LV's help. Judging by the response, so does the Love Vixen. Whoever Concerned Cuz is, she has it bad for her twin brother's best friend." Brianna glanced over at him. "Honestly, I cannot imagine ever being in love with any of your friends or Shane's," she commented, referring to her twin brother.

He had no proof, but he suspected plenty of Shane's friends had been attracted to Brianna over the years. And he knew some of his acquaintances had shown interest in her since she'd moved out to California.

"Anyway, Concerned Cuz says she hasn't seen the guy in a while, but her brother's wedding is coming up, and he's the best man."

His finger froze on the remote's arrow button. "Does the writer give any other details?" *Like a location?* "If she's looking for advice, that's not much for someone to go on."

"Let's see." Brianna scrolled back up through the comments on the page. "It says they kissed sixteen years ago, and she hasn't seen him since. The person wants to know if she should follow her plan and ignore him or make a move and see what happens."

Kissed sixteen years ago. The memory of the night he finally gave in to his desire and kissed Isabelle broke out of the ironclad box he kept it in. If he'd known that night would be the only time they'd kiss, he never would've done it, saving himself from years of having it torment him.

"What advice does the writer get?" There were probably thousands of women out there who had a twin brother getting married soon. And out of those, maybe hundreds who had feelings for their brother's best friend. Nothing about the comment stated it came from Isabelle.

But what if it was?

"LV tells her to go for it and stop wondering once and for all." His sister's cell phone rang, and she slid her laptop over to him as she grabbed it. "Here, read it for yourself."

Cameron waited until his sister left before glancing at the screen and reading the request sent in by Concerned Cuz. Statistics weren't his thing. In fact, he'd hated math in school, and if not for Bryson's help, he never would've passed any of his math classes in high school. But right now, he'd love to know the odds regarding how many people besides Isabelle and him could fit the situation described.

He read the response posted by LV. Yeah, his sister was right. The romance guru believed the author was also the one looking for help. And whether or not the person looking for help was Isabelle, he couldn't shake the belief she was or deny that the Love Vixen was right. Sixteen years was a long time for someone to be pining for someone—her choice of words, not his. Regardless of the outdated word selection, he knew how the person in question felt. Isabelle didn't know it, but he'd left his heart behind sixteen years ago, and ever since, he'd been wondering what would have happened if he'd called her as he'd promised.

What do I have to lose? Cameron raked a hand through his

hair and considered the question. For the past sixteen years, he'd gone out of his way to make sure his visits home didn't correspond to Isabelle's. On the rare occasions when they ended up on the island at the same time, he avoided any places she might visit and then left as soon as possible.

And why?

Because Bryson had asked him to leave her alone, and Cameron hadn't wanted to risk their friendship.

But his best friend had made the request a long time ago. Perhaps it was time to put Bryson's wishes aside and worry about his own.

Then, of course, instead of Isabelle being the person asking for help, it might be a woman living in Texas, and Isabelle might arrive at Bryson's wedding with a boyfriend. Although he rarely brought up her name, he wanted to believe Bryson or perhaps Mom would tell him if Isabelle was engaged.

Don't rush anything. He needed more information before he approached her. Thankfully, details about everyone's personal life were easy to obtain on Sanborn Island if you knew who to ask. "Be smart this time."

"First you're hanging around here on a Saturday night. Now you're talking to yourself. Do you want me to write the speech for you so you can get back to normal?" Brianna asked as she walked around the sofa and sat down again.

Lost in thought, he hadn't heard his sister approach. Although she didn't spend a lot of time there, Brianna had more friends on the island than anyone he knew. More important, those friends knew everyone's business. Hell, if he wanted to know if Mrs. Masters, his third-grade teacher who was now the elementary school principal, still ate peanut butter and banana sandwiches every day for lunch, one of Brianna's friends could find out for him. Yep, one of them would be able to help him get details about Isabelle if he didn't find them on his own.

"I might need some help. I'll let you know."

End of excerpt from One Of A Kind Love.

ABOUT THE AUTHOR

USA Today Best Selling author, Christina Tetreault started writing at the age of 10 on her grandmother's manual typewriter and never stopped. Born and raised in Lincoln, Rhode Island, she has lived in four of the six New England states since getting married in 2001. Today, she lives in New Hampshire with her husband, three daughters and two dogs. When she's am not driving her daughters around to their various activities or chasing around the dogs, she is working on a story or reading a romance novel. Currently, she has three series out, The Sherbrookes of Newport, Love on The North Shore, and Elite Force Security. You can visit her website or follow her on Facebook to learn more about her characters and to track her progress on current writing projects.

facebook.com/christinatetreaultauthor

twitter.com/tetreaultauthor

instagram.com/cgtetreault

OTHER BOOKS BY CHRISTINA

Loving The Billionaire
The Teacher's Billionaire
The Billionaire Playboy
The Billionaire Princess
The Billionaire's Best Friend
Redeeming The Billionaire
More Than A Billionaire
Protecting The Billionaire
Bidding On The Billionaire
Falling For The Billionaire
The Billionaire Next Door
The Billionaire's Homecoming
The Billionaire's Heart
Tempting The Billionaire
The Billionaire's Kiss
A Billionaire's Love, a novella
The Irresistible Billionaire
The Courage To Love
Hometown Love
The Playboy Next Door
In His Kiss
A Promise To Keep
When Love Strikes
Her Forever Love
Born To Protect

His To Protect

Love And Protect

One Of A Kind Love

Made in the USA
Middletown, DE
28 September 2022